THE ADVENTURES OF THREE OLD GEEZERS

The Bright Idea

Richard Perron

ISBN: 151525030X
ISBN 13: 9781515250302
Library of Congress Control Number: 2016920311
CreateSpace Independent Publishing Platform
North Charleston, South Carolina

ACKNOWLEDGEMENTS

First of all, and not to seem egotistical, I would like to thank myself for finishing this book, and not leaving it as just another unfulfilled idea, unnoticed when my yardstick of life runs out. Equally important I would like to thank Nora Butler for her ability to keep me on track, and for her insight and ideas which helped put this story together. Her abilities as an editor and proofreader were invaluable. Her faith in me brings a tear to my eye.

Cover by Phil Fisher.

CHAPTER 1

THE BRIGHT IDEA

I had only walked a couple hundred yards, when I could feel the first drop of perspiration sliding down the side of my face. It was warmer than normal on this early Saturday morning in May. Summertime had arrived early, and I was on my way to meet a couple of friends for the morning cup of coffee and the typical conversation that comes from those who don't have much to do. Pretty much the same scenario, day after day, after day. I was just rounding 12th Ave. South onto 3rd Street when the sun cracked the horizon. The sky had a surreal look - huge white mountainous clouds tinged with bright orange and yellow. Just breathtaking. Nothing like a good cup of hot coffee on an 80 degree morning with 90 percent humidity and a dew point of

77. A warmer than normal early summer day in southwest Florida. Walk a mile, sweat a quart.

I could see Frank and Bill down the street, sitting in front of Bad Ass Coffee. Frank had already lit a cigar. I could smell it in the heavy air. Bill was reading the newspaper. I hadn't read a newspaper or watched television for a long time. It was all bullshit and it was bad for you. As Mark Twain said, "If you don't read the newspaper you'll be uninformed, and if you do you'll be misinformed." Same with television, except the brainwashing power was stronger. I prefer to be uninformed. I know the truth is harder to figure out than what caused the big bang. Anyway, I knew the game, just not the players. Which corporations were ripping us off and who was waging war, and what politician was lying to us didn't really matter. There was nothing I could do about it. Big business runs the world these days. I have become the "Watcher." I think I'm an interesting, fun-loving, and adventurous person. Some people may think I'm a sarcastic, negative, grumpy old curmudgeon, but I prefer to look at myself as a realist, not living under some delusion about what life is all about. Most people believe that life is supposed to be the way they see it on television and read about it in the papers, but I know better than that. I truly believe that for most people, their reality, or what they perceive reality to be is full of misconceptions, delusions, and based on propaganda by the government and business to keep the ignorant masses quiet, uneducated, amused with trivia, watching sports, buying "Stuff" they don't need, and out of the way of those privileged few who are to be left free to run the world as they see fit.

Most likely, Frank and Bill were talking about the women they saw last night by the Naples Pier. The pier was where they liked to hang out around sunset, sitting on a bench by the restrooms. Those guys aren't stupid; they know all the women end up at the restroom sooner or later. They especially liked looking at the young ones, the ones they could only dream about these days. When you get into your sixties and you're retired, most of what you think about is past experiences, things you've done, things you wished you had done, and all the things you would like to do, but know you never will. As soon as I was within earshot of my two buddies, I heard them call out in unison.

"Hey Captain! How's it going? See you're still breathing!"

"Oh yeah!" I shot back, "No money down and twenty-five years to pay!" That's what a banker/real-estate developer acquaintance told me a few years ago during the real estate boom in Southwest Florida. He's doing five to fifteen now, but at the time he seemed like a nice guy.

I went inside Bad Ass Coffee, and got my usual small decaf coffee and raisin bagel, and headed back out to see if anything was new with Frank and Bill.

I sat next to Frank. I didn't mind his cigar smoke. It smelled pretty good, and I smoked cigarettes anyway, so it wasn't going to bother me. I've smoked cigarettes on and off for years. While in my forties I ran six miles, seven days a week, and played two hours of tennis six days a week, and didn't smoke or drink. Even so, when I turned forty-eight I had a heart attack, which came as a shock, as you can imagine. I had a 100% blockage of the left anterior descending artery, commonly called "the widow maker". They fixed me up with an angioplasty. A few months later I was visiting a friend in Key West, sitting at a bar and thinking about how I had been so good about exercising and not drinking and I still get whacked with a heart attack. So, I asked the guy next to me for a Marlboro and the bartender for a beer, and that was that. I'm still playing tennis, but no running, and I'm still drinking and smoking. I don't think my heart attack was directly related to smoking, although it probably didn't help, but more likely related to the war between my DNA and all those wonderful fatty things I ate most of my life. A lot of what we ate growing up was fried in bacon fat, and I can still remember my grandmother deep frying donuts in the morning, and boy were they good. There is always the principal of cause and effect, and the effect of that kind of eating eventually caught up to me.

As I looked at Frank, he was staring into the distance watching his smoke rings slowly ascend, maintaining their perfect shape in the calm heavy air. Frank is retired like I am, and migrated to Florida a few years ago. He moved here from New England, where for thirty years he had an outdoor hot dog cart. Right on Main Street. Rain, snow, sleet, hail, hot and cold, no matter what the conditions were - Frank was there selling his hot dogs. He was a hot dog entrepreneur. You had to admire him; he did what he had to do, and did it on his own. Put his kids through college and put off living until all his responsibilities were taken care of. He and his wife were planning to retire to Florida. He finally closed his little business and two weeks later his wife suddenly died. So he came to Florida alone, and depressed. He felt life had passed him by, and it was eating at him. It's never a good idea to wait for some time in the future to live your life; you have to get it while you can. He now survived off his social security and did a few odd jobs around town for some extra bucks. He was still in pretty good shape, not too overweight, but a little chunky, mostly caused by too many hot dogs over the years. I'm surprised he never had a heart attack. He was about six feet tall, and half bald, but he thought he still had a full head of hair because there was a little patch left on top. We didn't bug him that much about it. He had the warmest big brown eyes you've ever seen. I had a bulldog once that had the same kind of eyes. When you talked to Frank you felt he could see all of you, inside and out, and that he was listening to everything you said like it was the last words he was ever going to hear. He always had a slightly puzzled, confused look on his face. He was well read, in fact he had a college education, he was honest, and had an interesting insight into the human condition. You talk to a lot of people when you sell hot dogs on the street. In other words, he was fun to talk to, and a friend I could count on, which is rare indeed.

I said, as I sat down, "What's going on Frank?" With that slightly puzzled look on his face he answered, "Not too much Captain. Just watching my yardstick get shorter and shorter." All three of us looked at our life in terms of the length of a yardstick, and we were at the thirty-four inch line and counting. Can be depressing when you think about how many more coffees at Bad Ass there would be. And, is this how we want to go out... face down in a bagel? Life is getting down and I'm getting dirty - I've got till midnight and it's eleven-thirty. That undeniable fact is what the three of us are trying to deal with. Either sit around and wait for the end of the yardstick, or get your ass out of Bad Ass Coffee - and get it while you can. All three of us were thinking about the latter.

Bill was a different sort. He was a local. Born and raised in the Naples area - he was a true Florida Cracker. For most of his life he has been an artist, and for years he had a gallery in town, eking out a living, as most artists do. Very few ever become household names. Bill loved the tropics, and has painted a thousand pictures of palm trees, pelicans and the Naples Pier. Trying to please the tourists and the snowbirds who liked to decorate their homes and condos with local scenes. He saw himself as an artist who should be living on some tropical island in the pacific, but that dream had never happened. He said he wasn't married and didn't volunteer any information about any previous relationships and we didn't ask. We knew something strange had happened; we just didn't know what. He had a couple of kids living in different parts of the country. He was a good natured guy, with plump red cheeks and a white pony tail, which kept him connected with his old hippie days, and he felt it made him look more like an artist. He wore quite the tire around his midsection. Give him a red suit, and he would look just like the perfect Santa Claus, without the beard. He was always talking about losing some weight, and he walked a couple of miles a day, but if you eat five thousand calories and burn off two hundred, there's not much of a chance of losing weight. He had a real fondness for chocolate cake and ice cream.

Bill spoke up. "Another beautiful day in paradise."

But what he really meant was...*shit, here we go again, the same old thing.*

We had been talking lately, mostly in jest, of other courses of action we could take to alleviate the boredom and do something exciting before our yard stick ran out. We all wanted to do something crazy and the one idea that came up all the time was... *let's take a boat to the Bahamas.*

I'm a licensed boat captain, and have been running boats in the area for over 20 years. I knew I was capable of getting us from one place to another, hopefully without getting killed or lost. So that was "The Bright Idea" - except none of us had a boat - nor did we have the money to buy the type of boat we would need to pull this off. This is where it gets a little far out.

"Any more thoughts on our crazy idea?" asked Bill. A couple of days ago Bill suggested that we should just "borrow" a boat, without permission, for a few months and bring it back unnoticed. Sounds crazy, and if we weren't in Naples it probably would be. Naples was one of those places with lots of boats, both power and sail, that are rarely used. People come down in the winter and spend thirty thousand dollars to get their boat running, use it two or three times to putt around the bay, and then by Easter everyone is gone until next winter. It's not as crazy an idea as you might think to just borrow one and bring it back before the owner returns next winter. We definitely knew there would be some risk, but even if we got caught, we didn't think they'd put three old geezers in jail.

The biggest challenges would be in choosing the best boat, and getting the proper documentation. There was a pretty good chance we would get stopped by some law enforcement along the way, and we would have to go through customs in the islands, so having the correct paperwork was a necessity. Lots of boats are delivered to the Islands by captains, and it's not unusual for the owner not to be onboard - in fact that's the norm. Rich people don't travel on their boat to its destination - they fly there, hang out and look cool.

I had been thinking about the documentation problem, and I have a friend who works at the local yacht club, who I thought might have some helpful information. I told the boys that I was making some progress on the details, and should have something positive to report in a couple of days.

Just to give you a little more background information on Naples, Florida: We're at 27 north latitude, 86 west longitude, due west of Fort Lauderdale on the Gulf Coast, bordering on the vast Everglades and the beginning of the tropics. It's basically where civilization ends on the west coast of Florida. Naples is the wealthiest city in the U.S., with more millionaires per capita than anywhere, and by far the most anal retentive. Private jets come in as thick as mosquitos, and Bentleys are more common than Chevys. It's the perfect spot for the well-to-do snowbird. Thousands upon thousands of people come down here for six months to escape the brutal northern winters. Many of the houses are as big as hotels, and are only used a few weeks in the winter. Seems a shame, but that's what keeps the economy in this area going.

I met a young guy from Venezuela a couple of years ago whose first job was at a pizza shop, delivering pizza. At the time, he didn't speak much English. On his first delivery he pulled up to a big house with lots of cars, and walked right in with the pizza in hand, and immediately got thrown out. He thought it was a hotel, but it was just someone's house. That's what Naples is: lots of money and lots of egos trying to out-do each other. You also have the upper middle class that comes here to get away from the winters up north, living in gated communities on the outskirts of the actual city of Naples. One gated community follows another, each with its own golf course and the guy at the gate to let you in, giving you that sense of security that you are safe and protected, and in your own little world. Naples has over one hundred golfing communities, and thousands of condos everywhere. Everyone's grass is the same length at all times. It's a miracle.

Most of the locals don't play around or venture out much during season - too busy at their jobs, or just trying to stay away from the traffic. The road congestion is hard to avoid. As soon as Easter arrives, there's a great exodus - and I-75 is bumper to bumper with mostly midwest license plates heading back. I would swear that if you went to Michigan in February, you might not find anyone there... they're all driving up and down Route #41 in Naples, especially around five o'clock, looking for that earlybird special - martinis.

Naples has typically been a winter destination for mid-westerners. Interstate 75 comes down the middle of the country and I-95 is on the east coast. No one wants to get lost, and there was no GPS a few years ago, so the majority of tourists took the road most traveled. Things have changed some in the past twenty years, and the east coast has become less popular, especially since Miami turned into a third world country. Cuba used to be 90 miles south of Florida, but has recently moved north, and is now part of southeast Florida.

Naples is not part of the real world; it's like going to another planet where everything is wonderful - and a far cry from the general woes of most American towns and cities these days. In Naples, people are wonderful, life is good, and business is great.

CHAPTER 2
GETTING READY

I had to be very careful about approaching my acquaintance who works at the yacht club. I didn't want to give off any vibes about what my intentions were. Luckily, I was able to obtain some information on a couple of prospects, and having been around the docks for years, I had my eye on a few of my own.

There were four good possibilities. All of them were sailboats. We couldn't even think about a powerboat. Thousands of dollars in fuel and lots of potential mechanical problems. Sailing was slower, but we weren't in any particular rush anyway.

The top pick was a 42' Beneteau. I checked it out online and got the virtual tour. A real beauty. Like a floating Ritz-Carlton. If you're going to borrow a boat, which I like to call it - rather than stealing, it might as well be a nice one. This sailboat had lots of room below, and easy maneuvering topside. Heavy and very seaworthy. A boat you could go around the world on without going crazy or getting beaten to death by turbulent seas. I was particularly interested in this one because it hardly ever left the dock, and obviously was rarely used. I figured this boat was our best bet. If we left in early June we had at least five months before we had to be back.

One possible glitch was the yacht maintenance company which probably took care of this boat, and the chance they would notice it was gone. In our favor was the fact that in the tropics there is always a certain lack of follow through. Anyway, it was something I had no control over. We could only hope for the best. If we left in June and got back by the end of October all should be fine.

The boys and I have never really discussed our abilities at sea. Because I'm a captain they assumed I knew everything, but the truth is, I have never sailed a boat before. I had been sailing a few times, did a little steering, but had no working knowledge of the lines and sails, or the art of sailing. All the time at sea I put in to get my captains license was on power boats. Don't get me wrong, I'm not an amateur, but I'm not Columbus either, and how difficult can sailing really be, anyway?

The biggest problem left to solve was making sure we had the proper documentation papers, which meant we were going to have to somehow board this vessel and locate them.   Our only option would be to break in, in the middle of the night, on a clandestine insurgence just like you see on TV.   It sounded pretty exciting, and every guy really wants to do illegal things, but most don't have the balls to carry it through.   It was the excitement of doing something in the middle of the night and trying not to get caught.   It must be all the television we watched as kids.   There's no doubt about the great lure and magnetism which draws people to a life of criminal activity.   I'm not talking about purse snatching or robbing 7-Elevens, but serious, "classy" crimes.   Seems like bankers and people on Wall Street do it all the time and never get in trouble!   Sometimes it's the thrill as much as the loot that makes it irresistible.   We were getting excited!

Two days later we had a plan.

I had a canoe, which we would use for our approach. There was a small boat launch close to the yacht club that wasn't used anymore because it was so overgrown with mangrove trees that it was impossible to launch anything other than a canoe.   With only a couple hundred yards to our target, it was perfect.   All three of us would wear dark clothes, bring a few tools, and paint our faces black with shoe polish.   We're talking excitement!

The next night about ten p.m., we pulled up to the launch, which was hidden behind a little strip of shops and restaurants, giving us some extra cover.   We quickly unloaded the canoe and slipped it silently into the water. So far so good. Frank got in the front, Bill got in the middle because he was the heaviest, and I sat in the rear. Frank and I had a paddle and all Bill had to do was sit still. Two paddles later Bill just *had* to turn around to say something, and sure enough we were all sitting in about two feet of water. If you have ever been in a canoe, you know how easy it is to tip over, and three old geezers can do it in a second. Frank and I could have been upset and yelled at Bill, but instead we all started laughing until tears ran down our blackened shoe polished faces. All three of us looked like we had just come from a Halloween party gone bad. We emptied the water out of the canoe, got back in, and continued on. Lesson learned.

The yacht club had a night watchman. Sometimes I would see him on my early morning walks. I would walk down to the yacht club, all the way to the end of the dock and back, and once in a great while I would see him walking the dock, dressed in his uniform. That was in the early morning. I would bet that in the middle of the night he'd be dozing in front of the television. It wasn't a great paying job, and the yacht club was getting pretty much what they paid for. With the watchman in mind, we decided to paddle in a big circle to the end of the dock, staying out of his range of interest. There was no moon, and other than a few lights on the city dock off to our left, it was dark. *Very* dark.

We quietly paddled around to the end of the dock, which was furthest away from the yacht club, and pulled up silently on the starboard side of the sailboat, so no one could see us from the club. The plan was for Frank and I to get on the boat and Bill was to stay on the dock and keep watch. We were more careful getting out of the boat, than getting into it. There was more than two feet of water here, and one dunking a night is enough. These are floating docks, so they move up and down with the tide, which made it easy for us to get on and off. We got off one at a time, Bill being first. He took up his position about fifty feet down the dock, where he could see all the way to the yacht club. He was our early warning system. Frank and I boarded the sailboat.

The first problem encountered was the lock on the companionway heading down into the interior of the sailboat, but there were only four screws that held the lock in place. I didn't want to break the lock, because that would be a dead giveaway that someone had been here. It only took a few minutes to remove the screws and dislodge the lock, and we were in.

This was a half million dollar boat when it was new, and you would think people might take better precautions against theft, but the Naples Yacht Club, complete with a night watchman, gave boat owners a relaxed sense of security. I couldn't recall ever hearing about a boat stolen from the yacht club.

Once in, we quickly glanced around. The chart table was right there on the starboard side, I opened the drawer, and sure enough, there was the ignition key. Upon opening a brown leather satchel next to the key, I found all the documentation we could possibly want. This was truly a gift from our higher power. She must be on our side. Frank and I took a few minutes to look carefully about, taking mental pictures of the cabin. Then, after carefully replacing the lock, we slipped away without incident, and were safely back home before midnight.

All that remained to do now was to set a date, and do the dirty deed.

CHAPTER 3

THE DIRTY DEED

It was now early June and the time was at hand. We picked this night because there was no moon, and we wanted total darkness for cover. We packed up all we thought we'd need, which wasn't much. A few clothes, camera, cell phones - even though I'm not sure if they will work wherever we end up, my trusty .357 and a few boxes of shells, just in case we need a little fire power. Pirates weren't that big a deal any more in the Caribbean, but drug runners can be a problem. Taking a weapon may not be the smartest idea, but it made me feel a little bit safer.

Our plan was to leave here with as little as possible and stop somewhere in the Keys to stock up on food, water, etc. No use complicating things before we even get going. I've done all the research I can think of, especially what we would need to get through customs in the Bahamas, which is where we will most likely end up. In the short amount of time we had spent on the boat, I surmised there were lots of the basics on board. Rich people left nothing to the imagination, money not being an object. Most of what we need for sailing will be on the boat.

At ten o'clock we all met at my condo, about six blocks from the launch site. Each of us was equipped with one small backpack. We left the vehicles at the condo and walked the back alley to the canoe, which was already in the water and ready to go. We loaded what little we had, got in and pushed off. We were fully aware that this was not the time to tip over again. We planned to stick to the same routine when we got to the boat. Bill was to keep watch while Frank and I got the boat ready.

We pulled up to the starboard side again, and unloaded, which only took about a minute. Bill took up his position a little ways down the dock. I removed the lock again, and went inside. Frank was taking all the lines off, except one, and tying the canoe to the stern. We had to do something with the canoe, since we couldn't leave it behind. We would tow it for a while and then let it go, or sink it in an appropriate place. The sailboat had a dinghy of its own. I quickly went down to the engine room and turned on the fuel supply, and electric power, but decided not to turn on any lights yet, just in case anyone was looking our way. I was just about ready to start the engine when Bill came running up the dock.

"Someone is coming!"

There was nothing else to do but lay low and hope for the best. If it was the watchman, we could only hope he was a lazy one. I could see his flashlight waving back and forth as he walked slowly our way. Just as he got within fifty feet of us, or just beyond where Bill was hiding, he stopped, turned and headed back toward the yacht club. So much for my latest stress test - my heart was beating like crazy and sweat was pouring down my face. How embarrassing it would be to get busted before we even left.

I whispered to the boys. "Let's give him a few minutes to get comfortable in front of the television, and then we can leave."

After half an hour, when I figured the watchman was fast asleep, Bill climbed aboard.

Miraculously the engine started right up. Frank cast off the last line, and I put it in reverse and backed out of the slip. We came about and headed down the river.

Three crazy old geezers and one "borrowed" sailboat.

CHAPTER 4

ON OUR WAY

Frank was jumping up and down on the bow yelling, "No money down! You better get it while you can!"

I had to remind him we were still in the river and not yet out of harm's way. There was still the Marine Patrol, Sheriff's Office, Fish and Game, and the Coast Guard patrolling the water, although not normally at this hour. But you never know - better safe than sorry.

Bill was quiet; his eyes wide open, and looked a little in shock, as we all realized what we had done.

About two miles downriver we'll come to Gordon Pass, our entrance to the Gulf of Mexico. We just had to keep cool for a bit longer.   When we exit the pass we'll head south and hopefully be safely on our way. The sun will be up in about six hours, and at dawn we will try to figure out how to raise the sails. Hopefully, we will have a freshening breeze out of the east, which will carry us miraculously southward towards the Keys, where we will fuel up and buy what we need.

We entered the Gulf of Mexico, went out to the sea buoy, turned left to 89 degrees, and headed almost due south. Off to our port side was the Ten Thousand Islands, the largest mangrove forest in the world. All protected land for about ninety miles south of Naples, all the way to the Keys. Except for Marco Island and a few small villages there was nothing at all. Just mangrove islands, trillions of mosquitos, and Everglades National Park, home to everybody's friend - the alligator. Off to our starboard side was Mexico, seven hundred miles to the west.

Having put some distance between us and Naples, I decided it was time to cut the canoe loose. Someone will find it and have themselves a free canoe. We were moving along at about seven knots, which meant we would be in the Keys in about twelve hours. This gave us plenty of time to check out the boat, including the electronics, and get ready for our first stop. I put on the running lights, and started the generator for a little bit of cool air down below.

This was a fairly new vessel, and all pushbutton. The autopilot was a piece of cake, you just had to set the course and push the button that said auto pilot and that was it. The boat took you wherever you wanted to go. I turned on the chart plotter, which was a genius of a device. If Columbus had one of these he could have found the new world without even looking outside the porthole. The chart plotter was connected to the GPS, and in wonderfully bright colors showed exactly where the boat was within about three feet, also showing channel markers, water depth, hazards and anything on the shoreline you needed to know about. You could just look at that box and get anywhere you wanted to go. It was like a live video game. It only required that you put in the right chip for the area you wanted to wind up in, and everything you need to know is right there in front of you. Wow, it seemed so easy! The last thing to do was to turn on the radar. It's a necessity, especially out here at night. I put it on a ten mile range, and there was not a blip to be seen. Seems we were the only ones out here.

The three of us sat talking quietly together in the cockpit, still in awe of what we had just done. We were all a little afraid we had bitten off more than we could chew, and felt maybe we should just bring the boat back and forget all about this crazy idea.

Bill said, "Come on guys, this may be our last adventure… our yardstick is getting shorter, so what the hell, let's make the best of it and get it while we can!"

Frank and I agreed and we all decided to accept what we had done, and try to enjoy it. After all how many people our age steal a boat and head off to parts unknown? This was the chance of a lifetime, wasn't it?

The night sky became increasingly beautiful the farther away we motored. It seemed as though you could see every star in the Milky Way. When you get away from city lights and away from land, the view into the heavens makes you feel very small. It was truly a big sky tonight.

I asked Frank and Bill to go down below and see what they could find of interest or anything that could be of use along the way. After a few minutes Bill came climbing back out laughing, with a bottle of Captain Morgan spiced rum in his hand, with Frank right behind him.

"What the hell, let's have a couple of drinks to celebrate! There's no one around for miles and miles!"

So we started passing around the bottle. Frank lit a cigar and I smoked a cigarette. Bill didn't smoke, but he sure did like the rum. We talked about all the exciting and even dangerous things that might happen to us. It didn't take long before the rum was getting low and we began singing a song from the movie "Jaws". "Show me the way to go home, I'm tired and I wanna go to bed"… You know the song.

Frank got up and walked to the bow and was standing there like Leonardo DiCaprio on the Titanic, when suddenly the boat began to slow down, and then stopped completely and abruptly. The bow went down, and Bill and I fell to the floor of the cockpit. Frank, playing the Titanic role, continued on south, right over the bow and into the water, rum in hand.

I quickly moved to kill the engine, then jumped up to look for Frank, and heard him yelling, "I'm over here!"

I screamed back at him, and I could see him swimming for the stern. He swam around and I helped pull him back on the boat. The first thing out of his mouth was, "What the fuck was that?"

I knew exactly what the fuck that was - we ran aground! If a boat captain tells you he has never run aground, he is either lying or he's not a boat captain. Shit happens, and it's usually from negligence - basically not paying attention. Drinking rum and staring at the sky constitutes not paying attention.

It was mostly sandy bottom everywhere in this area, and it's doubtful we did any damage. The only problem would be if we had run hard aground at high tide, because if so, our situation would only get worse and most likely we would have to get someone to come and tow us off, and we definitely didn't want that.

I checked the tide table and luckily for us we were almost at low tide, so all we had to do was sit tight and wait for the tide to come in and we would be on our way again.

I knew we had about six hours to wait on the sandbar, and that was going to change our arrival time in the Keys. It didn't really matter though, we weren't in any rush. However, in these waters, close to the U.S. shoreline, danger lurked not far away. Florida has always been a great place for the importation of drugs. In fact, a lot of the charter boat fishermen in the Naples area got busted a few years ago when the DEA shut down Everglades City which is located just south of Naples, with only one road in and one road out, it was easy to close it off, and they proceeded to arrest just about everyone including the chief of police, and charged them all with smuggling.

The procedure was simple. The big boys would bring the drugs close to shore on large shrimp boats and the locals would go out in their fishing boats, pick it up and bring it the rest of the way in, where the boys on land would come and get it. The locals didn't sell it; they were just like mailmen, making a delivery, and being paid handsomely to do it. They knew their way around the back waters of the Ten Thousand Islands. It didn't take a genius to see through what was going on. All these local cracker fishing guys had new trucks and wore Rolex watches. There obviously wasn't *that* much money to be made in fishing. They just didn't have enough sense to keep it cool.

This same type of activity went on in Key West and other coastal cities. Miami was built on laundered drug money. Laundering money wasn't always illegal. Times have changed though, and there's a lot more law enforcement around now. Just outside of Key West are giant radar balloons suspended a thousand feet up that track anything moving on the water, or in the air.

There was also the illegal immigrant issue. With so many people from Cuba, Haiti and other third world countries desperately wanting to get to the U.S., it meant the Coast Guard was never far away. I didn't want to get paranoid about the situation - after all we did have good boat documentation and passports - and being three old geezers, I didn't think anyone would give us a second thought. That is, unless someone had noticed the boat was gone, and called law enforcement. A radio was much faster than we were. I just kept my fingers crossed.

Having a few hours with nothing to do we examined everything we could on the boat, from bow to stern. There were some extra parts, like impellers for the water pumps, fan belts, extra bilge pumps, some oil, and a small tool box for easy repairs.

This was one roomy boat, with the main stateroom forward with a private head, and two berths in the stern with a second head. The boys wanted me to take the stateroom since they looked at me as the Captain, and they both chose an aft berth. There was plenty of room for all of us. The boat was wide, a generous fourteen foot beam, which meant we didn't have to bump into each other all the time. Regardless of how big a sailboat is, it's still a sailboat - not unlike a trailer on the water, and you can get a little claustrophobic. Being able to go topside increased the space greatly.

We decided we should try to get a little sleep, while waiting for the tide to turn. I stayed up on deck and lay down, and Frank and Bill went below.

CHAPTER 5

OFF AGAIN

I could feel the boat beginning to rock and the warm morning sun on my face. It was time to head out, so I gave a yell down below and woke the boys. They both staggered topside, and we all realized this wasn't a dream. We were really on this boat and doing this crazy thing.

Bill, rubbing his face, said "I thought when I awoke I was still in a dream, but holy shit, here we are for real."

Frank nodded in agreement.

I started the engine and made sure I paid very close attention to the chart plotter and the depth indicator, and slowly headed for deeper water. This boat drew about six feet, and we would be fine if we just followed the normal route to Marathon. The chart plotter showed me which way to go, and the depth finder kept me in touch with the bottom. We headed west for a couple of miles and then turned south, back on course to Marathon. I put the auto pilot back on. We were still under motor power, but now we had time to look at the rigging and try to figure out how to put up the sails. I had checked this boat out on YouTube, where you could watch a video on just about anything you wanted to know. It's one thing seeing it though, and another thing actually doing it. But this was all pretty basic; just keep the pointy end of the boat in the direction you want to go.

I knew some of the terminology involved in sailing, but very little about sailing itself. I've been on sailboats a few times and was a little knowledgeable about what to expect - and of course being a Captain you pick up a things along the way. As far as hands-on sailing ability, I was definitely a beginner.

I questioned Frank and Bill as to the extent of their knowledge, and Frank said he'd had a Hobie Cat, as a kid up north. Bill had taken a sightseeing cruise on a catamaran in Naples when his kids came for a visit. Not much there to work with. We'd just have to make do.

The wind was coming from the east, which in this case was an off shore breeze, blowing from the land out to sea. It was just perfect for us as it involved no tacking about. We looked at all the lines and followed them from their origin back to the helm and figured out which one was for the main sail. There was a piece of canvas, like a bag, around the mainsail and we opened it, then wrapped the line around the winch, and started to crank. Sure enough, the main sail slowly rose up the mast, foot by foot, all the way to the top. I showed Frank and Bill how to tie the line off. So, without much trouble, we had managed to put the main sail up. The forward sail was curled nicely around its home on the bow and we followed the line back, wound it around a winch and cranked, and it unfolded like a champ which amazed all of us.

It wasn't critically important to know the names of everything, just how to use them. Figuring all this out was going to take some time, and time was what we had plenty of. For now, we were under sail, so I decided to kill the engine. This was a moment to remember. With the engine off we were moving along with nothing but the sound of the hull going through the water and the breeze blowing against the canvas. The feeling was wonderful.

I told Frank and Bill that I had a couple of friends that lived in Key West, and suggested we ought to go there instead of Marathon. Have a little fun, stock up, fuel up, and make our way from there.

Bill said, "Hey, why not? What difference does it really make? Marathon, Key West, Venezuela…what the hell. Let's do it!"

Frank quickly agreed. We made a small change in our course of a few degrees, and we were headed to Key West.

I determined that we'd be pulling in to Key West by about five p.m. I knew that our best bet was to get out of U.S. waters as soon as possible, but a little stop in the Keys should be okay. I could only hope and pray that nobody back in Naples had discovered the boat was missing.

I was aware of a small anchorage near the main part of town, about a mile from where the cruise ships docked, where we could anchor out. Mostly transients and people looking to save a few bucks hung out there. Staying at a marina cost up to two dollars a foot per night. We decided we'd drop anchor there, take the dinghy in, check things out with my friends in town, and figure out how to get provisions, fuel up, and get out of town.

CHAPTER 6
KEY WEST

Following the chart plotter's directions, we arrived in Key West about seven o'clock. We put the sails down, and made our final approach on engine power.

Sure enough, I saw the area we were looking for. Lots of sail boats and some power boats were moored near a small island.

I found a spot for us and dropped the anchor and made sure we were held fast. The anchor was a piece of cake. It had an automatic windlass, and with the push of a button the anchor descended. We just needed to put out enough scope to be held fast, but not so much that we could slide around and bump into another boat. I was familiar with this routine on power boats, so it was no problem.

The next challenge was the dinghy, which was held over the stern by a small davit. It was an Avon Inflatable with a ten horsepower Evinrude motor. It was simple enough to see how the davit operated. Just a button for up or down. A push of the button and the dinghy slowly dropped down to the water.

We took the lines off, and secured it to the boat. Next we had to try to start the motor, which could present a problem. The company that maintains this yacht would be responsible for making sure that everything aboard worked properly. I hoped the dinghy was included as part of their protocol.

I got in the stern and pumped the ball that sends fuel to the engine. I gave a couple of yanks on the starter cord, and lo and behold, it started right up.

Bill got in carefully, and then Frank, and we were off. I knew a little bit about the lay of the land, because I've been here so many times. There was a place I remembered where the dinghies tied up and we headed for that. We tied on to another dinghy and climbed over a few more until we got to the dock. So far so good.

We were headed first to find Harry, my old friend. Harry is married to my tax accountant, Martha. As a professional musician, he's been playing guitar for years around Key West, but mostly at the Pier House, a fancy hotel at the end of Duval Street, right on the water. It wasn't much of a walk. Frank and Bill were up for anything at this point.

There were people swarming everywhere, which wasn't unusual for Key West - a true "party town" at the end of the road - the very southernmost point in the United States.

Many dysfunctional people end up here, trying to outrun their shadow. However, you can put a monkey in a box up north and ship him to Key West, and when you open the box there's still a monkey inside. Wherever you go - *there you are.* I'm sure most of them figured that out sooner or later, or died trying.

The bartender at the Pier House told me that Harry was playing at the Hog's Breath Saloon tonight, which was not far away, so off we went to find him.

What a name: *Hog's Breath.* It just had to be successful with a name like that. I think they do several million a year in T-shirt sales alone, aside from the food and beverage sales. All the tourists want a souvenir from Key West, and Hog's Breath is one of the hot spots.

We got closer to Duval Street, the main drag and home to a multitude of T-shirt shops, bars, and restaurants. The entire street was a litany of tourist traps. There were motorcycles everywhere, mostly Harleys. The street was closed to automobiles, and we couldn't't miss the huge banner hanging over the street that proclaimed: "Welcome to Bike and Dyke Week!!!"

Wow! I had forgotten about this crazy festival, and couldn't believe our timing!

Years ago I had owned a Harley, and had made quite a few trips to Key West during Peterson's Poker Run. The ride started in Miami and ended in Key West. A poker run is an event with five stops along the way, and you pick up a card at each stop, and at the end of the run, the highest hand wins. There were probably twenty thousand bikers who came out for this run. Not everyone participated in the poker run, most just came along for the ride and the experience.

There were a lot of gays and transvestites in Key West, and we happened to arrive just in time for the transvestite parade. All these guys dressed up like women… it was quite the sight, but nobody cared. It was all for fun, and down here no one cared what you did, as long as you didn't bother anyone else. That's why people come here. Bikers and gays together, so what? They were all crazy, and reveled in it.

Bill said, "Wow - lots of weird people here!"

I answered, "You should feel right at home."

Who wants to be called normal, anyway? Here, you could be yourself, no matter what that was. This was a dangerous place, if you wanted to live here and not go crazy. There were plenty of drugs, including the all-time favorite - alcohol - and plenty of people who did it all. Some survived and some didn't. This was not a place to cure a dysfunctional personality. It was like throwing gasoline on a fire.

Key West has its good points, one being the weather, and the other being the crystal clear beautiful water - and if you loved to sail, fish, or dive, there wasn't any place better. On the down side, there wasn't any place to go, just one highway on and off the island. It was small, and at the very end of the road. If a hurricane was on its way, an early departure was well advised. The whole island was barely above sea level, and flooded very easily. You can hide from the wind, but you can't run from the water. A hurricane in Key West would have similar results to what had happened in New Orleans. It wasn't the wind that killed everyone, it was the tidal surge. I guess every place has its good and bad points; you just have to decide what you're willing to put up with.

There was a sense of excitement here. Lots of music, crazy locals, tourists up the ass, cruise ships coming and going, and more bicycles and scooters than you could shake a stick at. Tourist towns always give one a feeling that there are good times to be had.

We didn't stay long at the parade. We were on a mission, and soon headed straight to the Hog's Breath Saloon, which was just one street over. The saloon is open to the street and as we got closer I could see my friend Harry, singing away, sitting on a small stage off in one corner. Harry was one of the survivors here. He and his wife Martha have lived here for over twenty years. Martha has taken care of my tax reports, and Harry and I have been music buddies.

Harry has made somewhat of a name for himself as an accomplished singer and songwriter. He has a few CDs out and has developed quite a following. Some of his songs are even played on Margaritaville Radio - Jimmy

Buffett's satellite radio station. He also does a lot of touring about in the summer, so he gets away for several months a year, which is probably how he keeps his sanity. Twenty years ago he worked for the Democratic Party in New Hampshire, which is where I'm from. He was a speechwriter, and he also played the guitar. Hard to believe, but I was a florist at one time, and we met one another through the floral shop business that I owned, across from the State House.

We became friends because he came in my shop quite often to buy roses for his fiancée Martha, and we shared an interest in music.

One cold, snowy day he said to me, "I'm quitting my job and heading to Key West to play music."

I said, "Wow! Where's Key West?" Being from New Hampshire you tend to be quite isolated from the rest of the world and unaware of the variety of lifestyles. At least I was. This move he was making was in the mid 80's, before Key West gained its national notoriety as a place to go and get crazy.

He said, "It's at the end of the road down in the Florida Keys."

I had to look it up.

I admired his bravery and sense of adventure. I'm sure it wasn't an easy decision. It's scary to get rid of just about everything you own, hit the road with your guitar, and start a new life. I gave him fifty dollars for a few sets of strings and wished him good luck. I've heard it said that most people live lives of quiet desperation. Was I one of them? Inside, I wished I had what it took to do something like that. I didn't know it then, but not many years later I would have my chance.

Frank, Bill and I went inside and grabbed a small table near the area Harry was playing, ordered some beers, and waited for him to catch sight of me. I'm sure I was the last person he expected to see. A few minutes passed and his eyes met mine, and I could see the surprised look on his face. It had been probably a year or longer since I had been down this way. He sang two more songs and then announced his break, and hurried over to our table.

"Hey Captain!" he exclaimed, followed by a big hug. "What a surprise! Why didn't you tell me you were coming!?"

"It's a long story, I'll tell you later. It's great to see you, your music sounds great! Where's Martha? Can we give her a call and get her down here?"

"Sure," he said, "I'm sure she would love to see you. Are you going to be here long?"

"Not any longer than I have to", I answered with a meaningful, sly look. "I'm on the run, but I'll explain it all later."

I introduced my friends, and he phoned Martha.

Harry had a beer with us, and invited me up on his small stage to play a song.

Maybe I didn't mention this, but I'm also a singer and songwriter, and have been playing the same Gibson guitar for over forty years. I played professionally in my younger days, and still do a few gigs in Naples. I play with a crazy bass player; in fact, they say all bass players are crazy. I play mostly my own original music. It never made sense to me to be a songwriter and play other people's music. I do a few old popular standards, but mostly just want to play my own. I have a few CDs of my best songs, and a small but loyal following. We mostly play for small events, or for various groups that enjoy hearing what I play. I've had my fill of bars and restaurants. The money I make probably keeps me in coffee for the year, but that's okay these days.

I decided what the hell - I might as well get up and see what happens. You have to get it while you can. What did I have to lose? Harry gave me a little introduction, handed me his guitar and it was showtime! I said a few words into the microphone comparing the difference between Key West and the anal retentive city of Naples, where I live. People who come here want to have a good time and let it all hang out. It's as far as they can get from their normal experience. They love original music, and there is plenty of it to be had around this town.

I started the song, and after only a couple of bars they were all clapping to the hard beat, so I knew they understood about music, and then they were all up on their feet. Wow, it was such a rush! I won't sing the whole song for you but the first line goes: "It's Friday night and what you gonna do? You're goin' downtown to Fifth Avenue... where the girls are all lean and lookin' to be seen...they're looking for that money machine!"

Fifth Avenue was the hot spot in Naples, like Duval Street was in Key West, except they're different as night and day. I finished the song and they all went crazy clapping and screaming for more. I know it's always best to leave them wanting, so I took my bow, handed the guitar back to Harry and sat down. Frank and Bill were in awe, they had never seen anything like it, and frankly neither had I.

Harry returned to the stage, and we boys called for another round of beer.

Martha showed up a short time later, gave me a big hug, sat down and ordered a fancy drink with an umbrella in it. I thought it was a little touristy for her, but what the hell. I made the introductions, and she asked me how the drive down was, and I told her we were on a boat. She asked what kind of boat it was, and who owned it. It was too early to tell her the whole story. I just said we borrowed it from a friend, and had the use of it for a while. Martha was one of the few sane people in Key West - she didn't get carried away with all the craziness. After some heavy partying upon her initial move to Key West she soon settled down to a reasonable lifestyle, just going crazy once in a while. She is a CPA with a great sense of humor. Imagine that! She's attractive, and very personable. Her greatest attributes were her sense of humor and her ability to put up with Harry. That's why they were still together. She let him do what he wanted, even if he wanted to spend six months playing music around the country. Harry made pretty good money from his playing, but he spent a little bit more than he made, so Martha was the financial foundation in this relationship. She made the money and kept it all together. Somehow they've made it work.

We chitchatted for about an hour and Harry played his last song for the evening. He didn't have to pack up because he was playing the next night, so he suggested we go for a bite to eat at Blue Heaven. I've eaten there before and it's one of the best restaurants in town, maybe anywhere. We piled into his van and off we went.

Blue Heaven, made famous in a Jimmy Buffet song of the same name, was not in the best section of town, but we didn't care. We found a place to park not too far away. Upon entering, the first thing you notice is the dirt floor. We were shown to a table underneath a huge banyan tree. There's no roof over most of the place, and it's like eating under the stars. Martha wasn't drinking umbrella drinks now; she requested a Captain Morgan and coke, which was my favorite and what I was drinking. Bill and Frank wanted a shot of Tequila, and I thought, oh boy here we go, so we all had a shot. I made a toast to good friends and an exciting future. As we toasted we noticed the chickens in the tree; in fact one walked right under the table. I ordered chicken (!) and another shot of tequila for all.

After dinner, (and by the way the chicken tasted really fresh), and several more shots of tequila, we could hardly get up from the table. There was no way we were going to make it back to the boat. We would be lucky to make it back to the car. Martha suggested we stay at their house. I've stayed there quite a few times. Their house was a stilt home with an enclosed lower level, housing her office and a small apartment, and they lived upstairs. It was small, but cozy, with several other cottages enclosing a quaint tropically landscaped compound, with a big swimming pool in the middle. Most of the houses in Key West are tiny, but very expensive. It is the most expensive real estate in the country per square foot. Frank and Bill crashed on the lower level and I fell right to sleep upstairs on the couch.

I could feel the warmth of the morning sun coming through the window, and I'm usually awake before sunrise, so I knew it was time to get up. Martha was making coffee, and Harry was taking the dog for a walk. I went downstairs and woke the boys. They weren't very interested in getting up, but with a little coaxing they began to stir. I'm sure there was still a little alcohol flowing in their veins. About a half hour later, the boys were up and ready, Harry was back from his walk, and Martha suggested we go to Pepe's for breakfast.

I've been to Pepe's before, it's the oldest bar and restaurant in town. There were a few tables inside and a small bar and tables outside. We chose outside of course. The floor was made of old brick, wavy like the ocean and trees growing up seemingly right out of the brick. The specialty here was Mimosas, which is champagne, orange juice and a strawberry on top. The orange juice was fresh and hand squeezed. I could see the bartender squeezing the oranges, yum! We ordered breakfast and I began to tell Harry and Martha what we were up to. Their eyes got bigger and bigger. I tried to convey the fact that we had a plan and it was thought out as much as it could be. There were a couple of rough edges, like relying on the hope that no one would notice and report the boat as missing. She thought we were all crazy, and I couldn't disagree. I think Harry was about to ask if he could come along, but knew it wouldn't go over well as he had responsibilities. They filled us in on where we could fuel up and buy groceries. Their suggestion for these errands was over on Stock Island which was the next key up the chain. It was a small place, mostly local fishermen and crackheads. Nobody there really cares who comes and goes.

The biggest business on Stock Island was the tattoo parlor. You would think in Key West there would be tattoo parlors everywhere. Tattoos are very popular these days, but for some reason there was a law banning tattoo parlors in Key West, so everyone went to Stock Island for their tattoo. Harry volunteered to come with us, and make sure we at least got started off on the right foot, so we left Pepe's and headed for the dinghy. Martha gave me a hug, wished us well, and made sure to tell us one more time she thought we were all crazy.

CHAPTER 7
STOCK ISLAND

Somehow, all four of us managed to fit in the dinghy, and slowly made our way out of the small harbor to the boat. When Harry first saw it his reaction was one of surprise. "Wow, you guys sure know how to do it up right!"

"Yeah", I said, "if you're gonna borrow a boat it might as well be a nice one!"

Harry is a sailor, and has done a lot of sailing around the Keys, so on our way to Stock Island I planned to pump his brain as much as I could about how to manage the sails. He'll impart lots of information which will really help us figure out how all this rigging worked.

We headed around the west end of Key West and into the Atlantic. On one side of Key West - the north side of the island - was the Gulf of Mexico, and on the south side was the Atlantic. We stayed as close to the shore as the depth of the water would allow, and headed east up to Stock Island. The trip only took an hour, and we dropped the sail and motored into a small channel.

If you like Old Florida you'd like this place. Crab-traps lined up on land, alongside old boats whose days on the water were over. Lots of old trailers, and basic houses, built many years ago in the easiest and cheapest manner. Time and sun have taken their toll. At this point, maintenance was a useless afterthought. Not many people made a lot of money in this town, and it showed. Weathered almost to death, it was populated mostly by those who couldn't afford to live in Key West.

We motored up to a ramshackle marina, and were met by a guy who looked like he had spent most of his life in the sun. He was skinny as a rail, had brown leathery skin, and a few strands of hair sticking out from his baseball cap. He was probably much younger than he looked. Too much sun had a way of making you look older than you really were. His raggedy clothing appeared to be purchased from the local goodwill store, many years ago.

He gave us a friendly shout, and waved. He had a line in his hand, ready to throw to Frank, who was standing on the bow with Harry. Frank grabbed the line and Harry showed him how to properly tie the line off on the cleat.

"What can I do for you guys?"

I replied, "Fill 'er up with diesel."

We asked where the nearest grocery store was, and he directed us to a small IGA a few streets over. We grabbed a dock cart and off we went.

At the IGA we had to figure out what we really needed to hold us over until our next stop. I had no idea where our next stop would be, but Harry had suggested we head for the Turks and Caicos, which is a chain of islands in the southern part of the Bahamas. It would keep us away from the heavy boat traffic around Bimini and Nassau, and afford us a little bit of cover. I had thought of going to Cuba, but between Florida and Cuba were lots of eyes keeping track of the comings and goings of boats. Maybe Cuba would be a good idea later, when we could approach it from a different direction.

We grabbed as much bottled water as we could. Can't live without water, and the water already aboard in the fresh water tanks may not taste very good anyway. We got a few pounds of sliced ham, roast beef, chicken, a few cans of tuna, and some peanut butter and jelly. Five loaves of bread, and of course butter. We also got some canned goods, like Dinty Moore Beef Stew. Several boxes of pasta and some spaghetti sauce, along with a few candy bars, some orange juice, and grapefruit juice. That seemed like enough. Bill did mention we should get some fresh fruit so we wouldn't get scurvy, so we picked up a bag of key limes. They would go great with the rum. We'd probably forget something, but this was enough to keep us going for a while. There was also plenty of fish we could catch along the way. Last but not least, was a supply of rum. Whatever the question is, the answer is rum. There was a small liquor store next to the IGA, so we bought a case of gallon bottles. Running out of water was one thing, but running out of rum would be a crying shame.

With everything loaded in the dock cart, we headed back to the boat.

The fueling was finished. We only took fifty gallons, but at six dollars a gallon, that's a fair chunk of change. According to the information on the boat, the tanks hold three hundred gallons, which at one gallon an hour we could motor pretty much anywhere we wanted to go. I filled the fresh water tanks, while Frank and Bill put everything away on board including a few bags of ice. I bought some oil and some oil filters. We paid for everything with cash. I thought it would be best not to use our credit cards for a while. We kept track of all our expenses, and at some point, we would sit down and figure out who owed who, and how much.

CHAPTER 8

THE ATLANTIC

Martha was on her way to pick up Harry, so he wished us well. I could tell he wanted to come with us, but the timing just wasn't right, and besides what we were doing wasn't legal. Possibly lots of trouble down the road. We motored away from the marina and out into the Atlantic and headed southeast. There was an offshore fifteen knot breeze hitting us just aft of the port beam, which made it perfect for sailing a straight course. We put up the sails, turned the engine off, put the auto pilot on and sat back to reflect.

All three of us were pretty quiet for the next couple of hours, just a little idle chit chat. I felt scared and happy at the same time. We have done something people only talk about. I think most people only talk about the lives they wish they could live; rarely do they actually act on their wishes. Leaving the safety of comfortable surroundings generates fear in most humans. The status quo is always safest. Fear truly rules most people's lives. I know it did mine, and I couldn't be much different than most other people. I think that's why I respected Harry so much; he swallowed his fears and took that step. He dared to make that leap of faith. There are always risks, but the rewards can be great. The three of us were reaching out now, and stepping into the unknown. Better late than never. We could all wind up in prison - or be set free from our uneventful lives.

I have always been an entrepreneur, and with that comes the willingness to take risks. Why I had to be in business for myself I'm not sure, maybe I didn't like taking orders from anyone else, or maybe I enjoyed being in control of my own destiny, but I suspect it was the fear of getting a job.

I owned several businesses over the years, but by far the most successful was my florist shop. The job of an entrepreneur is to find a niche or a hole, and fill it. There was already a big florist in town, but it seemed to me there was plenty of room for one more. I liked flowers and plants. The only problem was I didn't know anything about the business, but that wasn't going to stop me. I did what I needed to do to figure it out. I took a risk and it paid off.

After several years my wife became tired of the flower business, and wanted to sell it. My lawyer was hot to buy it for *his* wife. How naive is that? He thought it would be fun for her. All he saw was my new Porsche, and all the pretty flowers. He made me an offer I couldn't refuse. To make a long story short, he bought it. I retired at forty eight, and left for the Keys with my wife. My lawyer's wife never worked in the flower shop, and they sold it a year later.

I spent the first winter of my retirement in Key West. My wife and I spent four months with Harry, and a couple of weeks in Naples, which we discovered on the way to the Keys. It was my first awakening to the fact that there were lots of different lifestyles out there, and a shitload of very rich people. I believe my wife had an awakening also, and after arriving back home from our winter in Naples, she announced, "I don't love you anymore, I've filed for a divorce, the sheriff is coming tomorrow, and I've split up the money."

There's not much you can say to that. Two weeks later she had new breast implants and was off to Florida, where apparently she thought the grass was greener. Little did I know at the time that it was the best thing that could happen to me. This turn of events would also mean the eventual end of my retirement. A half of something is not quite as good as the whole.

The next winter I came to Naples again. This time life took an unexpected turn and put me on a totally new path. After tennis one day I was riding my bike down by the docks and there was a guy sitting there reading a book. He started up a conversation, asking me what I was up to. I said, just playing a little tennis. He asked me if I wanted to do some mating on his charter fishing boat. Casting my fears aside, I said why not? I wasn't doing anything and besides I'd a boat of my own for years, although not as grandiose as this one, and I had done a lot of lake fishing up north. Sometimes you have to step outside of your fears and take a shot. After a few months he suggested I get my Coast Guard License, and run a one hundred forty passenger tour boat he was going to purchase, and suddenly my life was on a new course. I eventually sold my house in New Hampshire and just about everything I owned except for my guitar, and a few clothes. I packed it all in a VW Golf, left the safety of comfortable surroundings, and headed off to a new life as a Charter Boat Captain. I took the leap just like my friend Harry did a few years ago. There I was, living on the edge. It just might be true that everything happens for a reason. When you least expect it, POW!!

My mind returned to the present moment, and I felt relief that everything so far was working out just as planned.

We were all sitting in the cockpit, still in awe of what had taken place.

Frank said, "I feel just like I did when I was a kid, when I stole my old man's car in the middle of the night and went for a little joy ride."

"We've all done that," said Bill.

"Not all kids steal their parent's car and go for a joy ride at night", I said. "It takes a special person to do that. Most kids do crazy things when they're young, at least I hope so. I feel sorry for the ones that didn't."

Bill chimed in, "I still feel like a little kid. Everything looks the same as it did when I was little. We all enter the adult world and have to act a certain way, and that's just what it is, an act. We're all kids at heart, and all that growing up stuff is just a bunch of shit. Responsibility... fuck that! I want to play cowboys and Indians again, and run around in the woods." Spoken like a true artist!

I replied, "Sure, and if we get caught we can plead the Childhood Syndrome. I'm sorry your Honor, we just haven't grown up... Our defense will be the curse of the nine year old. I'm sure he'll understand and let us go home to mommy."

Frank interrupted, "Look at the color of that water! Wow! I've never seen that color blue before."

That's the color you get when you're in really deep water. "It's called the *deep blue*. As I understand it, the light is scattered when it hits the water and the deeper the water the bluer it is. The red part of the spectrum is reflected off and the blues travel deeper. The color of the water also has to do with what's in it, like algae, and the type of bottom. You'll see when we get to the Caribbean how the water will change in color, and we're gonna have to understand these color changes if we don't want to run aground every day. We have the chart plotter, which is great, but if something happens to it, we're going to have to have some idea of what we're doing." Some of my nautical knowledge was coming back, and it felt good.

Just as I finished my dissertation on the color of the water, a blip appeared on the radar screen, about five miles off to our starboard side, which would be southwest of us, and heading our way pretty quickly. The shipping lanes were in this area and we had seen a couple of cargo ships heading west, either up into the Gulf of Mexico, or continuing on through the Panama Canal and on to the west coast, but this blip was moving fast, and it was small, much smaller than a cargo ship. In about a minute I could see a gray shape coming into view and I grabbed the binoculars.

This boat was steel gray with outboard motors. It didn't look like a recreational boat. I've been fishing in the Keys a few times and recognized this as either the Coast Guard or the DEA. Either way, this may become our first encounter with the law, and I had no idea whether they were looking for us or not. Normally they will scope you out from a distance, and make a determination to approach or just let you go on your merry way. Maybe they were bored and wanted to harass someone, or maybe they were looking for a stolen sailboat! I informed the boys what might happen, and what might not. If they do come up to us, try to be cool and act like you're having fun. Law enforcement on the water doesn't need probable cause to board your vessel. They can do whatever they want and there is nothing you can do about it. Just be friendly, keep your mouth shut, and do what they ask.

They kept coming, and when they were about fifty yards from us they hailed us on the VHF radio, which was always on channel sixteen, the hailing and distress channel. I answered, and they asked me to come about, and I responded with a Roger. The water was fairly calm, and we quickly lowered the sails, trying to look like we knew what we were doing, and I reminded the boys to keep their mouth shut and let me do the talking.

They pulled up right alongside, and they looked like nobody you wanted to mess with. On the bow was a mean looking fifty caliber machine gun. These guys were armed to the hilt with automatic weapons. Drug runners didn't give up easily, and were also heavily armed. It could turn real nasty for these guys and they looked prepared to win. Their boat was the biggest center-console vessel I had ever seen. It had to be at least forty feet long and powered by four 300 horsepower outboards. Not many people could outrun these guys.

They put some bumpers out and tied up to our side.

"Good afternoon, gentlemen," said the Head Honcho. "Where are you boys from, and where might you be going?"

I quickly replied, "We're from Naples, Florida and we're heading for the Turks and Caicos Islands."

I figured there wasn't any sense in lying. They either knew about us or not.

"Are there any problems in the area we should know about?" I asked, surprised by how calm and nonchalant I sounded.

"Nothing unusual, just doing our job. Lots of drug runners and people trying to get to the U.S. illegally. We just check everyone out and try to make sure the area is safe."

He asked me a couple more questions about nothing in particular, but he did want to know if there was anyone else on board.

I said, "It's just three old geezers trying to get away for a while".

Much to my relief he said, "Okay. You three old geezers have a good day and stay safe."

They pulled away from us and sped off and were gone as quickly as they came. We were giving each other the high five, jumping up and down.

I said, "It's five o'clock somewhere - lets break out the rum! We've just passed our first test!"

CHAPTER 9
NIGHTTIME ON THE ATLANTIC

We had survived our first encounter with the law. It was obvious that no one had reported the boat missing, unless they just hadn't heard about it yet, but I'll go with the former. To celebrate, we had a couple of rums with freshly squeezed lime juice (don't want to get scurvy), and we were all feeling quite content. We were far from the sight of land and the sun was setting. The breeze was dropping off and we decided to lower the sails and motor our way along. We had enough fuel to motor for days if we wanted to. Frank went to the galley to make sandwiches for all of us.

It would be dark shortly, and we needed a plan for the night. We couldn't travel through the night without having someone on watch. You never knew what you might run into out here. There were other boats like us, and also large commercial ships moving about. Floating debris was another potential problem.

People think the ocean is a great place to dump stuff, like plywood, trash and whatever else might fall off these big ships. The chances were slim of hitting something, but the chances are also slim of getting hit by a falling coconut on land, but shit happens. The fact is, more people are killed by falling coconuts than by shark attacks. Out here, you have to be prepared. The chart plotter showed where the main shipping lanes were, and we had one more to cross.

We had to split up the night into three watches, lasting four hours each. Since there were three of us, one of us would be on from eight to midnight, and the next from midnight to four and the last, four to eight. We drew straws and Frank was the first up, then Bill, and I drew the last watch. I told Bill he might want to get some sleep and I tried to impress upon them both how important it was not to fall asleep on watch.

I put the running lights on. The running lights are a way to be seen and to determine which way someone was going. They help to avoid collisions and determine who has the right of way. How many masthead lights would tell you how big something was, and the green and red side lights would tell you along with the stern light which way someone was heading. You could tell if they were coming at you, going away or heading to the left or the right. The lighting configurations were part of the rules of the road, and it's amazing how many boaters have no idea what they are.

I was sitting in the cockpit with Frank when I heard Bill call up from below,

"Hey guys, I think we forgot something!"

"What's that?" I said.

He yelled loudly, "Toilet paper!"

Frank and I started to laugh, although it was a bit of a situation.

"We didn't get napkins or paper towels either, so just use your left hand like they do in some parts of the world!"

"That's really funny, ha ha, but it wouldn't be so funny if you were down here."

"I'll come down and get you one of your T-shirts and you can use that and some water from the sink.

Just rinse it out off the stern and hang it on the back of the boat."

I said loudly, "Forty percent of the world's population doesn't have indoor plumbing and probably doesn't have four-ply Scott toilet paper hanging around."

Bill yelled back, "Yeah, but forty percent of the population isn't sailing around on a yacht, where you would most likely find toilet paper. Hurry up!"

I ran down and got him a T-shirt and before long we had one T-shirt hanging up off the stern. I told Bill and Frank they might want to stay away from the Dinty Moore beef stew. That could be a two T-shirt cleanup.

I was getting tired, and the sun was ready to set, so I thought I would have one more rum and turn in. Frank's watch had already begun, and I reminded both of them again that it was REALLY important not to fall asleep.

I have a great inner clock and I woke up about ten minutes to four. I was climbing up the ladder and into the cockpit, and I could see Bill lying there, out like a light. Just as I stepped into the cockpit I heard it, and turned to my left and saw a giant wall, black and sinister, moving straight for us. I dove for the wheel and turned as hard as I could to port. The wall continued to come, and I thought surely this is it, all of this just to drown at sea. We were pushed up by the leading wave. The wall just grazed our stern and continued on with Bill's shit-stained T-shirt stuck to its side. Bill was awake now and screaming at the top of his lungs, while Frank was trying to climb up the ladder. You could hear the deep low frequency of the engines and the huge propellers spinning around. It was the biggest thing I have ever seen. It must have been a thousand feet long, and if it had hit us it was doubtful they would have felt a thing. The big oil tanker finally went by us and we just sat there looking at each other. Bill was very apologetic, going on and on about how sorry he was. We told him we forgave him. We were just lucky my inner clock was working, and we weren't at the bottom of the sea. Another lesson learned.

Frank and Bill went back down below, and I took my watch. I doubt they went right to sleep. I was definitely wide awake. I sat there the rest of the night looking at the sky and pondering the fate of the universe and three old geezers.

CHAPTER 10

A NEW DAY IS DAWNING

No one slept very well during our first night on the Atlantic. We had narrowly escaped disaster, like a squirrel almost being hit by a truck. I was sitting alone topside and watching the sun come up, while trying to keep positive thoughts in my head. It can be depressing to think I'm now just an old geezer, whose yardstick is getting shorter, and heading to who knows where, on a boat I've stolen. How do I get positive feelings out of that? I'm trying to remember some of the things I've learned over the years, like gratitude. I reminded myself that I'm in pretty good health, and I've got friends, and I'm doing what I want to do even though it may not be on the up and up. Life is pretty exciting right now. I can feel it and see it all around me. Maybe I'm doing better than most people. So there, I'm feeling better now. A little gratitude is all you need. It just depends on how you look at things.

A short time later, Bill and Frank came topside. We sat around in silence for a few minutes, each wondering what was next.

I said, "Let's put up the sails and do some sailing." In a minute the sails were up, the motor was off and we were in heaven. I reminded Bill he'd need to get another T-shirt, that his was stuck on the side of that oil tanker, and on its way to parts unknown. A couple of hours later there were three T-shirts hanging off the stern. Life is good.

It was a perfect day, with a fifteen to twenty knot breeze pushing us along nicely. The seas were about four feet and we rode the swells easily.

Frank said, "I love all that stuff we bought to eat, but here we are in the middle of a giant fish bowl, and there are fishing rods down below. I saw some lures we can use, so why don't we see if we can catch a fish. What do you think? We can throw a line off the stern and do a little trolling."

"Great," I agreed, "Let's get it on."

We were really feeling like little kids now. We have stolen the cookie jar and now we are going fishing.

Frank and Bill rigged up the lines, and threw them over the stern. They let out about fifty yards of line and put the rods in the rod holders. All we had to do was sit back and wait for a hit. I had no idea what was in these waters. Maybe there was nothing, but we were about to find out. We were doing about nine knots, a good trolling speed, so whatever hit the lure should be a pretty good game fish. At least it gave us something to do and helped keep our minds occupied.

When you're out on the open sea there really isn't any clock, it's either day or night, and keeping that in mind we broke out the rum. We were just sitting back enjoying the serenity of the situation when there was a *click, click, click* on one of the reels.

All of a sudden the line began zipping out and I yelled, "Let down the sails!"

Bill and Frank both jumped to action. I started the engine to keep us moving forward and give us some maneuverability. Frank went back and grabbed the rod, put his feet against the rail and his back against the cockpit.

"On the next run set the hook really hard," I instructed. When the fish took the line again, Frank wasted no time in setting the hook - and bombs away - this fish was heading for Mexico.

"Easy Frank! Let him have line, but tighten up the drag a little, and put some pressure on him."

Over the next thirty minutes, Frank was pushed to his limit, and had to hand the rod off to Bill. This fish was powerful and soon Bill was at his limit, too.

"I think he's coming up!" I screamed with excitement. "Make sure you keep tension on the line!"

Sure enough, in a few seconds the fish broke water, and flew into the air. It was the biggest fish we had ever seen. It looked bigger than the fish The Old Man and the Sea had caught. It shimmied out of the water, throwing its head from side to side, trying to free itself, but Frank had set the hook firmly. Bill held on to the rod as long as he could and then I took over. Another half an hour had gone by and I was pulling hard, trying to gain on him. Slowly but surely he was getting closer to the boat.

I yelled to Frank, "Get the net!" Frank grabbed the net and stood on the stern. I pulled up on the rod and reeled down, again and again, bringing him closer every time. Soon we could see a dark shape in the water. I reeled like crazy, and brought the fish within eight feet of us. When it saw the boat, off it went like a shot out of a gun. Ten minutes later, I could feel it was finally getting tired. It was losing the fight, and Frank was ready to do his part. We could see it now. It was huge, and shone iridescent in the sun.

Frank was shaking his head, and warned, "There's no way this fish is going to fit in the net!"

I yelled, "Get the gaff!"

Frank ran for the gaff and when the fish was right off the stern he quickly inserted the gaff under one gill, and pulled up on it. Bill had to help lift it on board. It was a beautiful tuna, and it wasn't about to give in yet. It thrashed violently on the deck. Bill finally just sat on it, and it slowly calmed down. The fish was absolutely perfect, and I had a moment of guilt. I felt bad about killing him, but that was the way of the world.

With the fish finally quiet, I took a fillet knife and took two giant fillets off, one from each side, and threw the fish overboard, where it would become part of the food chain.

There was a gas grill on the back of the boat and it didn't take long to fire it up. I put the fillets on the hot grill. Two minutes later I flipped them over, and in another two minutes they were done. It was just like eating butter. We all agreed it was better than anything we'd ever tasted. Smooth and delicious. This was truly *fresh* fish. We ate till we couldn't swallow another bite.

"Wow!" I said, "What a great day."

We sailed on, and as the sun set we took our turns at watch.

I was sure no one was going to fall asleep this time.

CHAPTER 11

SECOND DAY ON THE ATLANTIC

This would be our second day on the Atlantic, and we needed to start thinking about where we are actually going to go. We had some early ideas about our destination, but out here things can change as quickly as the weather. We had plenty of charts on board and it was time to get them out. I had done some research on the possibilities of going to Cuba, but the politics and red tape involved didn't seem worth the hassle. The Caribbean was the best and safest place for us to hang out. There were hundreds, no *thousands* of islands, many of them uninhabited. My chart plotter indicated that soon we were going to run into one of those little islands.

Mid-afternoon, as I was studying the charts, I heard Frank yell loudly, "Land ho!" For a moment I thought I was on some sailing vessel from the 1500s. I moved quickly topside and spotted the land, dead ahead, and only about six miles away from us. I knew what it was. It was Flamingo Cay. I had seen it on the chart plotter, and knew we were on course for it.

Just a tip for those who like to get it right. *Cay* is pronounced: Key.

We had left the deep blue some time ago. Now the water was a beautiful turquoise color and the depth was only about ten feet which meant we only had about four feet underneath us. Time to be careful. We have already run aground once, so caution was the word of the day. We anchored up about three hundred yards off shore, lowered the dinghy and headed for the beach.

This was our first experience on a Caribbean island. We beached the dinghy on sand that seemed as pink as the Bazooka bubble gum I use to chew as a kid. The sand was made from tiny pieces of coral, and when you picked it up and dropped it back into the water it sank like a rock. It was heavy and did a great job of massaging your feet as you walked along. There were a few palm trees, but mostly just low scrub brush. It wasn't the flora and fauna that gave this place its charm, it was the coral reef and the crystal clear water, and the rich, deep indigo blue sky.

We made a quick decision to spend the night on the island. I stayed on the beach and Frank and Bill went back to the boat to get some food, drinks, and some bedding. There wasn't any sign of rain, as would typically be the case during the late summer afternoons. I scouted around for some firewood, and a good place to bed down. It didn't take the boys long to get back with the necessary items for our beach camp out.

Bill said, "Maybe you didn't notice back at Stock Island that I bought some hot dogs, and tonight we can cook them over an open fire and relive our youth a little. Frank replied, "You know me and hot dogs...if I eat one, practically my whole life flashes in front of my eyes."

"That's great," said Bill, "We can all have some flashbacks, but first - it's five o'clock somewhere. Let's break out the rum."

We had a couple of rums each, cooked some hot dogs over a fire and then decided to take a little stroll around the island and see what we could find.

It was obvious other people had been here before. There were remnants of other fires here and there, and some didn't look very old. There were a few bottles scattered about and lots of sea glass dotting the sand.

Bill said, "Why don't we take a little souvenir from everywhere we go? Just to give us something to remember from all these places."

I said, "Good idea. This place has plenty of sea glass and pink sand, let's take a little of each."

Most of the island couldn't have been more than a few feet above sea level. Only a small part of the eastern end of the cay was high, rising up about thirty feet. I'm sure during a big storm most of the island must disappear beneath the sea. Kind of like our little adventure - we were washing away the past and making a fresh clean start.

We came over the top of a small sand dune, and could see the other side of the island. The whole cay was only about the width of a football field.

Frank said, "Hey! Look over to the right just a little. I think I can see some black boxes high on the sand."

As we got closer it became clear that these boxes had been put here and stacked neatly up.

I said, "I know exactly what these are. They're called *square grouper.*"

Frank naively asked, "Why are they called square grouper?"

"That's a nickname, after the fish. They get thrown overboard by drug smugglers when they're being pursued by the cops. You can still find them floating in the Gulf once in a while. In this case, looks like someone has left them here to be picked up later, by themselves or someone else. They could be filled with pot or cocaine."

Frank said, "What if we took just a little, and tried to sell it later on? Maybe we could make a lot of money!"

I replied "Yeah, maybe we could make a lot of money, and maybe we could end up dead in the process. I don't think this is anything we want to get involved in.

I'm fine drinking rum, plus we're already in pretty deep as it is, with the stolen boat. Why add drug smuggling to the charges? Somebody is probably going to come looking for this stuff before too long, so I say let's leave well enough alone and mind our own business."

We all agreed, and walked back to our campsite.

It was one of those amazingly clear nights when it seemed you could see every star that existed. We were drinking rum and cooking more hot dogs over an open fire on a deserted island in the middle of the Caribbean Sea. Our choice of transportation: a stolen sailboat. This is definitely not an everyday experience. I'm sure there isn't anybody the three of us know who would ever be in this situation.

I suddenly spit out what was hanging around in the back of my mind.

"What if somebody comes back tonight for their stash and here we are sitting around eating hot dogs, and see them? They may not be too happy about that. We may not want to, but I think we should pack up, go back to the boat, pull anchor and put a little distance between us and this island."

Frank asked, "What do you think the chances are of that happening?"

I responded, "What were the chances of us being where we are now?"

We all agreed to pack up and leave, and within ten minutes we were on the dinghy, heading back to the boat. It didn't take but a few minutes to pull anchor and be on our way.

It was a calm night, so we didn't bother with the sails. There was a small cut of deeper water a couple of hundred yards to the east and we headed for that.

We had only motored a few miles away from the island when a blip appeared on the radar. I looked through the binoculars and I could see the lights of what appeared to be a small boat moving quite fast, not intersecting our course, but heading in the direction of the island we had just left. I had no way of knowing who was on the boat or where they were going, but I had my suspicions.

In an hour we had gone another five miles, and a new blip appeared on radar. This one was much closer to us. A small boat traveling pretty fast, heading straight for where we had just come from. It had a red hull and looked like one of those boats from Miami Vice. They passed close enough to see us clearly. They didn't stop to say hello.

Seemed like it might be a busy night on our little island. I was glad we were on our way.

CHAPTER 12
A SHOT IN THE DARK

A couple of hours passed and Bill was on watch. Frank was asleep, and I was lying on my bunk still thinking about the island and the two boats we saw earlier headed towards it. All kinds of scenarios were playing out in my head, when Bill poked his head down the hatchway and quietly said, "There's a blip on radar, coming along fast, about four miles behind, and heading straight for us."

My heart started beating faster and my brain was whirling around. Those two boats that went by us had left me with some inner discomfort.

I woke Frank up, quickly filled him in, and went topside to take a look. I could see the boat's lights and I told Bill what I was thinking.

"If something went wrong back at the island and that first boat had taken the drugs, these guys might think it was us."

Bill with that typical worried look on his face said quietly, "What should we do?"

"I don't know what's going to happen, but they're probably armed and not looking for a cup of tea and light conversation. Frank, you stay up top with Bill - maybe they'll go right by us and nothing will happen. I'll go below and be prepared for whatever happens."

Bill turned with an anxious look on his face.

"What are you going to do?"

"I've got my .357 in the bilge area and I'm going to get it out and be prepared to use it if I have to. You don't want to die out here do you?"

Bill yelled, "Jesus Christ, how can this be happening to us?" Are you sure you know what you're doing?"

"No, I'm not sure! If you've got a better idea, let me know real quick!"

I hurried back down the companionway, got out my trusty .357, and turned off the cabin lights. I positioned myself in the darkness at the foot of the ladder where I had a good view of Bill and most of the cockpit area. Within minutes, I could clearly hear their engines as they came alongside. Suddenly, I heard an agitated voice saying something to Bill. I couldn't make out what he said, but I could see Bill put the boat in neutral and we immediately slowed to a crawl.

Bill gave me another worried look. Frank was out of my view, but I knew he was just behind Bill, on the port side, away from the approaching boat.

I could hear Bill call out, "I don't think that's a good idea. There's no reason for the gun - we don't have anything you want."

The loud voice asked how many people were on board, and Bill nervously replied.

"It's just the two of us."

The next thing I know, a tall skinny guy was standing on our deck, with a gun pointed straight at Bill. I could see a tattoo on his arm. He demanded to search the boat.

Now you can wait for life to happen, or you can make it happen, and this was a time for the latter.

I took close aim at his gun, took in a deep breath, let it halfway out, and slowly squeezed the trigger.

It was like the shot heard around the world. My head seemed to explode, just like the round leaving the chamber. The gun flew out of the man's hand spinning him sideways, propelling him over the railing, and into the water. It was a miraculous shot. Just like in the movies.

Frank and Bill hit the deck and I charged up the ladder. My immediate concern was how many other assholes I'd have to contend with. As I reached the deck I instantly looked towards the other boat where I could see a second guy reaching for something, probably another gun, so I fired one more time into the air and screamed at him to put his hands up where I could see them. Luckily, he did.

I shouted to Frank, "Get aboard, and see if you can find any other weapons while I cover you!"

Frank jumped on their boat, found another gun, tossed it overboard, and returned.

By this time the man's cohort was climbing out of the water and up onto the transom of their boat, seemingly unharmed.

I called out loudly to the two of them, "We have nothing that would be of interest to you. We didn't start this shit, but I'm going to put an end to it."

I thought to myself, *I don't really want to kill these guys*, but I couldn't just let them go. I made a quick decision.

"You guys have some pretty nice engines there, twin 300's. Must've cost a lot of money. I hate to do this."

I fired a round into each engine. They were screaming at the top of their lungs. I knew that without power and being far from land, they were going to be floating around for quite a while. They could call the Coast Guard on their radio, but under the circumstances I was pretty sure they wouldn't do that, and besides their boat was probably stolen. Most likely their radio was out of range of any friends back on land.

I told them I knew what they were looking for, and that we didn't have it. I informed them about the boat we saw earlier that passed us before they did, suggesting they were most likely the ones who had stolen their stash. I also said in no uncertain terms, "If you try to find us again, I won't be so kind."

I asked Frank to get a case of water and toss it on their boat. Bill put the engine in gear, and we slowly moved away into the night, their pleadings fading in the distance.

CHAPTER 13

GRATITUDE

Bill and Frank were jumping up and down, screaming *"No money down and twenty five years to pay!!* (Our favorite saying.)

Bill said, "Holy shit Cap, that was incredible! I've only seen that done in the movies!"

I quickly retorted. "Well I wasn't always a florist or a musician... there are some things about me you don't know. Anyway, what was I supposed to do? Let them shoot us?"

Frank said, "There wasn't any way around it - you did what you had to do. Who knows what they might have done to us!"

I suggested that we should alter our destination. If we stayed on our present course, we could be asking for trouble. Especially since the eight knots we were doing wasn't exactly speeding.

After looking at the chart we decided to head to Georgetown. It was a small island in the Exumas, and a port of entry for the Bahamas. We had to get this immigration situation over with and the sooner the better. This would take us on a radically new course, and hopefully keep us out of harm's way. Somebody might be looking for retribution.

All three of us had gotten a pretty good look at our smuggler buddies. The one who came aboard was young, and reminded us of the kid that played the banjo in the movie Deliverance - too many close family ties. He was sporting a tattoo of a snake on his arm. His partner-in-crime was an older geezer - like us. A little weatherworn, wearing a Boston Red Sox baseball cap and a scraggly white beard. Hopefully we wouldn't run into them again, but it's a small world, and in these islands it's even smaller. It was still a beautiful night so we got out the rum. After all, it's not like we have to go to work tomorrow.

"Ok Cap," said Bill. "Fill us in on all this James Bond action. Where did you learn how to shoot like that?"

"I was in the Marines, I answered, which you knew already. But what you don't know is that I was in a special combat unit and had a lot of training in how to kill people. I went to Vietnam, which I don't talk about much. It's not full of happy memories. I went places and did things I'm not exactly proud of. It was a long time ago, and some things they taught me I didn't forget."

Bill said, "If you don't want to talk about it, I understand." He continued. "I was in the Army, but before that I enlisted in the Marines. I was sworn in and scheduled to go to basic training in a couple of weeks. Before I left, I was out in the woods shooting twenty-two's with my best friend Tom. I was walking through a tunnel which went under a highway, and Tom hadn't entered the tunnel yet, and for some reason decided to fire a shot down the tunnel. The bullet ricocheted off the tunnel wall and ended up in my arm. He wasn't being very careful, obviously. Anyway, I had some nerve damage and the recovery time was a few months. In the meantime the Marines, for some reason, gave me a discharge, and then I was drafted into the Army. I ended up in Germany for two and a half years, working in an office building, smoking hash, taking an occasional LSD trip, traveling around Europe as much as I could and generally wasting my time. The irony of the story is - if my friend Tom hadn't shot me I would have ended up in the Marines, and Cap, you know where I would have ended up most likely...right where you were in Vietnam. Over fifty thousand guys came home in a box. I'm sure we all know someone who died in that crazy war. Here's the thing: My friend Tom ended up in the Army as a paratrooper, went to Vietnam and was

killed. Now, how crazy is that? I think he saved my life.
Sometimes it's hard to figure out why things happen the
way they do."

Frank said, "Wow, that's quite the story. I'm a little
younger than you guys and by the time I was of draft age
they had the lottery system. I had a high number and
was never called up. I guess I was just lucky."

"We were all lucky," I said. "Each in a different way.
Just look at us now! Here we are sitting on this stolen
sailboat, floating around the ocean. I don't think any
of us could have imagined we'd be doing something like
this. We should be very grateful for what we have."

We all shouted, "Amen! No money down...and twenty five years to pay!"

CHAPTER 14

GEORGETOWN

Georgetown was about one hundred and fifty miles away, and at the eight knots we were going, we'd have about a twenty hour trip. I looked at my watch and noted the time: *2 a.m.* We should arrive about ten o'clock the following night. We had the perfect breeze. Usually the wind dies down at night, but that night it was blowing an easy fifteen knots, and we could travel just as fast with the sails as we could with the engine. Fuel wasn't cheap in the islands, so why not use Mother Nature when you can. We cruised through the night, each of us taking a short watch.

The sunrise was spectacular, and we were all feeling somewhat elated that we had made it this far without any big catastrophe. All that had taken place so far was maybe just par for the course. Running aground;

meeting the DEA; nearly being run over by an oil tanker; and getting accosted by drug runners. Not a bad beginning, but I definitely hoped it would get easier from here on out.

As the morning progressed, we developed an appetite for fresh fish. We put some lines in the water and trolled for a while. Caught a couple of fish, and had a great lunch of grilled dolphin. Not the Flipper type - but *mahi mahi,* commonly called dolphin.

I knew we would arrive in Georgetown late that evening. I decided we should anchor some distance offshore and deal with customs in the morning. I needed to think this through, and be sure all was in order. We needed everything to look perfect. I hoped the fact that we were just *three old geezers,* would ease any suspicions.

CHAPTER 15

CUSTOMS

In the morning, we pulled anchor and headed for Georgetown. It was another beautiful day, and we were all hoping for clear sailing through customs and immigration. I put up the yellow quarantine flag. This flag told everyone that you were coming from another country and hadn't gone through customs yet. It was part of the protocol. We also had a Bahamian flag on board, so I knew this boat had been here before. We flew that flag also, as a courtesy.

On our arrival, I contacted the local marina on channel sixteen, and asked for dockage. They directed me to slip four. On board, we also had coast pilots for the Bahamas, another clue that this boat was no stranger to these waters. The books gave all kinds of information about the Bahamas, including marinas.

I found slip four and we pulled in and tied up. Next to us, on the T-dock, was a yacht that had to be one hundred feet long. She was beautiful, and spic and span. There appeared to be a crew of at least six aboard it, running around like ants on a teaspoon of sugar.

I told Frank and Bill that I was going up to the dockmaster's office to announce our arrival, and they were to stay on the boat. No one was allowed off the boat except for the captain, until you cleared customs. At the dockmaster's office I was met with a friendly face. He had fairly dark skin, a round face and a pleasant smile. He welcomed me and asked what he could do for me. I replied that I was the Captain on the boat in slip four that just arrived from the U.S. and needed to clear customs. He told me he would notify the authorities and that I should go back to the boat and wait there and they would be along shortly. I did as I was told. I was also aware that in the Bahamas, you might as well throw your watch away. There is a time called Bahamian Time and it means "sometime", and "sometime" could be *any*time.

I went back to the boat and got the documentation papers ready to go and our passports out. I had my Captain's license on hand as well.

About two hours later the customs and immigration guys showed up. They wore white shirts with some insignias above the pockets, and the customs guy had some yellow bars on the shoulders. They looked very official. One was skinny and one was fat. They looked like a comedy team, except these guys weren't funny at all. They asked us the typical questions, about where we were coming from and what our business was in the Bahamas. I told them we were from the U.S. and traveling to the Turks and Caicos Islands to deliver this sailboat for a friend, and then we were going to fly back to the states. I showed him my Captain's license.

We were asked if we had anything to declare, such as weapons, or certain fruits and vegetables that weren't allowed. We answered no to everything. We each had to fill out some paperwork and pay a couple hundred dollars for the privilege of stopping in the Bahamas. The money also included a fishing permit.

The customs guy was looking closely at the documentation, and I was holding my breath, waiting for him to say something was wrong. I was beginning to sweat, and probably looked nervous. After what seemed like an eternity, he looked up at me and said, "You guys look okay. Have a good time in the Bahamas!"

They said their goodbyes and climbed off the boat. I just about fell over. I couldn't believe we had done it. Made it through the most dangerous part without a hitch. We were permitted to travel throughout the Bahamas without worry. Life was good for three old geezers.

CHAPTER 16

TO SUM IT UP

It was the middle of August, and we had traveled all over the Bahamas. We'd caught and grilled every kind of fish, and snorkeled every reef in the chain. We had even eaten some authentic and delicious conch chowder under the bridge in Nassau. We were very tan, and we had all lost quite a bit of weight. I had to admit though, we were tiring a bit of this life on the run. In a way, it was becoming as mundane as the life we left. The grass always looks greener in your neighbor's yard, but in reality it's the same everywhere. Having something to look forward to is a true gift, and having something *different* to look forward to is the real key.

When you do something like what we were doing, and expect everything in your head to change, it never happens. It's true that *wherever you go, there you are*- and that happiness comes from within and not without. In truth, we were all missing our simple life back in Naples.

We decided to head for the Turks and Caicos Islands and then make our way back home. We planned on being home sometime around the middle of October.

It was about a ten day trip from where we were, but we wanted to continue poking around for a while, before heading back.

CHAPTER 17

CAPTAIN'S MOUND

It was smooth sailing all the way to the Turks and Caicos, and we stopped frequently to enjoy small uninhabited islands. We camped out under the stars many nights, feeling like we were the only people in the world. What was going to be about a week's sail took us three weeks. It was already the first week in September. We'd met a lot of people on this trip, and gotten a lot of tips about where to go. There is a town in the Turks called "Captain's Mound", which captured our interest, so we headed that way.

It was a small town, like most towns in the islands were, but this one was geographically higher than the normally flat terrain. Apparently, a lot of crazy people hung out there and that's what we liked - the crazier the better. The town was about the size of four football fields, and loaded with small bars, some only seating five or ten people. There was lots of music, some good and some bad, like anywhere. It was a great place for itinerate types and drug runners - and not much law and order.

The three of us were sitting in a small crowded bar overlooking the bay, a hundred or so feet below us. The bar was about thirty feet square with the bartender in the middle. Benches were lined around the perimeter. No windows, it was completely open to the weather.

We were on our third beer when Frank looked startled and suddenly said, "Don't look now - on the other side of the bar there's a young guy I think I've seen before. Does he look familiar to you guys?"

Both Bill and I took turns glancing casually over to the other side of the bar.

Bill said in a low voice, "Holy shit. I think that's the young kid that boarded our boat with the gun!"

I recognized him instantly, by the tattoo on his arm that I had stared at so intently, and reminded the boys about the tattoo. No sooner had the word "tattoo" come out of my mouth, than his partner - the old guy, strolled in and sat down next to him. He had a woman with him. Not bad looking, but she didn't appear too happy.

Bill grabbed my arm and almost fell off his stool. With a high pitched squeak, he said, "That's Julie, my goddamn wife!!! I need to talk to her!"

I quickly said, "Wait, wait, wait... what the hell do you mean *your wife?* Let's get out of here and talk about this. Don't start some shit in here!"

I put some money on the bar for the tab and we slithered away quickly, and hopefully unnoticed. We stopped close by, where we couldn't be seen, and I asked Bill for a little deeper explanation on the situation.

He reluctantly replied. "I never told you guys about this. I was ashamed, I guess. Shortly before I met you guys, my wife just up and left. I thought everything was okay, but obviously she didn't. She took most of the cash and I heard through the grapevine that she ran off with some boat captain- drug smuggler from Everglades City. She definitely thought the fish were biting better somewhere else. I can't explain what she did, but there she is! And she's not looking too happy!"

Bill, now with tears in his eyes, continued, "I just don't know. Life seems too complicated to figure out. Let's see what happens when they come out. I need to talk to her!"

We waited undercover, in the darkness. About an hour and a half later the three of them came out of the bar - the two guys staggering slightly. We heard Bill's wife say something to the older guy and he grabbed her hand and pulled her along, her resistance obvious. We followed them at a careful distance, down the hill to a small cove where an old houseboat sat, which looked like it could sink at any moment. The boat was tied up to some mangrove trees and it was almost beached. It had a small plank that went from the boat to the beach.

These guys were definitely losers. We sat silently, within earshot, in the shadows of the mangroves. The young guy came out to take a leak, and the old guy followed. They began quietly arguing about what they should do about the woman. Seems they still had some of her money, which they evidently planned to use for one final drug buy. By their conversation, they felt she knew too much about their operation. She had become a liability and they had no use for her anymore. The old guy said he would take care of the situation tonight.

Bill muttered angrily, "I'm going to get that bastard before he does something to Julie. I've got to get her out of this situation before they kill her and she disappears into the Atlantic. I need you guys to help me." Frank and I agreed we'd help. We couldn't just leave Bill all alone to handle the situation. I whispered to Frank that he should go back to the boat and get my .357, while Bill and I kept an eye on the situation.

We could hear loud talking on the boat. Frank was back in twenty minutes with my .357. I felt a little safer with my buddy by my side. The noises from the boat got louder. After a short time all was quiet.

We had to think fast. I told Frank and Bill that I was going to sneak up onto the boat and when I was hidden on the bow one of them was to throw something at the side door. Bill was adamant about coming, so I told him to take up position on the stern. As quietly as we could, we walked the plank - so to speak, and made our way onboard. I crawled to the bow and Bill to the stern. I waited a couple of minutes and gave Frank the high sign, and he threw a handful of shells at the side door. Sure enough, someone came out, and I could hear them heading for the bow. I stood up, gun held high, and a figure emerged right in front of me. I came down hard on the top of his skull and he went down like a rag doll, but not quietly. Almost instantly I heard the other guy yell *what the hell are you doing,* and before I knew it Bill hit him like a torpedo and flattened him to the deck. He tried to get up and Bill hit him again, really hard in the face, and down he went again. This time he wasn't moving.

Bill immediately went inside and I followed, and there was Julie, tied up and gagged on the couch. Her eyes got bigger than a hoot owl's when she saw Bill. He carefully removed the duct tape covering her mouth. All she could mumble was, "*Bill, Bill, Bill ... how, why... I'm so happy to see you... I'm so sorry!*" She was sobbing loudly. He told her to be quiet, that everything would be okay. He untied her and helped her up and we headed for the door. Frank had already dragged the old guy to the bow, where his buddy was still out cold.

I said, with a smile on my face, "So, we meet again. I told you I wouldn't be so kind the next time. Two things I want from you, and maybe I'll let you live. My friend here, who happens to be Julie's husband, would rather make shark bait out of you and your asshole buddy."

He looked startled and pretty scared this time.

I said, "Karma can be good or bad, and right now it's not looking good for you."

I put my trusty .357 right under his chin, and spoke in a low threatening voice.

"Here's how it's going to go down. Either you die, your buddy dies, both of you die, or *nobody* dies. It's up to you. Here's what I want: The money you have left of Julie's. I want it right now, or things are going to be very unpleasant for you."

He whimpered and said, "We don't have any money."

That's when I pulled the hammer back on the .357. It's a *verrry* intimidating sound.

I whispered to him, "I really don't care whether you live or die, and I don't really give a shit about the money, it's just a matter of principal. You've got three seconds."

In the blink of an eye he said, "Okay, okay. Inside, under the sink is a small leather bag. That's all I have."

With the most sinister look I could muster, I said, "If you lie to me you won't be happy."

Frank went inside and in a few seconds came back with the bag. Bill opened it and there was quite a bit of cash inside.

I asked the loser, "How much money is in here?"

"There's about twenty thousand, but that's not her money", he whined.

Bill said, "It is now."

The young tattooed guy was beginning to stir and I told Frank to find something to tie these guys up with. It didn't take but a few minutes to tie up the two screwballs. The young kid woke up and had nothing to say, but he looked mighty scared. He was definitely just a follower.

"The second thing I want," I continued, "is to be sure we never see you guys again. Now how am I going to be sure about that?"

The old man said, "Don't worry... I've had enough of you guys, *and* the woman. If I ever see any of you again it will be too soon."

I cautioned him, "If I should see you again, or hear you're back in Florida, my .357 will do the talking. If I don't kill you, Bill will."

I told Bill to untie the houseboat and I went inside. I opened the engine hatch and fired one round into the small diesel engine, and three rounds into the floor, which I'm sure, went right through the bottom. We quickly got off the boat and pushed it into deeper water. We hurried away from the scene, and for the second time I could hear their pleadings fading in the distance.

Bill said, "What do you think will happen to them?"

I replied, "It depends on how creative they can be, and besides, I don't really give a shit."

We made it back to the boat and quickly decided our time in the Bahamas was up. In fifteen minutes we were on our way.

Three old geezers, and one old geezer's wife.

CHAPTER 18

HOMEWARD BOUND

We quietly motored on for about two hours. I was up top with Frank and Bill, and Julie was resting down below. It had been quite a night for all of us. We decided to take it easy and relax, so I killed the engine and lowered the anchor. It was another one of those beautiful nights and a good time for reflection. No one had said much since we left. It was definitely time to get out the rum and loosen some lips.

Julie was up and about now, and volunteered to make some sandwiches and cut up some limes for the rum. Franks eyes were wide open, and Bill was fidgeting about. I could only assume there was way more going on in his head than he could make sense of.

He nervously asked, "What do you think is going to happen to those two assholes?"

"I wouldn't worry about them," I sparked. "They got what they asked for. I'm pretty sure they'll survive.

There was only about three feet of water where we pushed the boat off, so even if it sank they might get damp, but they wouldn't drown. I just hope they were smart enough to take a hint, and besides look at the result - we got your wife back!"

Bill, fumbling with his words said, "Yeah, yeah... we'll see how that works out!"

Frank chimed in, "Holy shit Bill, think about what just happened! It's another fucking miracle! Better chance of getting hit by a falling coconut out here. It must be fate. Just relax and see what happens. Who knows... we all make mistakes. I think you're still in love with her, and I think she really loves you. She sure was happy to see you! Take some time; it will all work out just the way it's supposed to. Bill nodded in agreement and simply said, "Yeah."

Julie came up from below with the sandwiches, limes and rum, and a giant smile on her face. She seemed relaxed, and glowed in the moonlight. She was a pretty woman, obviously a few years younger than Bill, athletic in her stature and tall - about five foot six. Fine classical lines on her face, with high cheek bones and bright green eyes. Her skin was slightly tanned and smooth. She must have done her best to protect herself from the sun, which was hard to do in this part of the world. Her hair was the color of carrot cake, and short. She was still pretty hot, but must have been a real knockout when she and Bill got together. She was also an artist, like Bill, and if you know anything about artists, they're not like most people. Their brains are wired differently. You might say they're flighty. They don't easily fall into a regimen like most folks.

I suggested we all take a shot of rum, maybe two, just to take the edge off. Pretty soon everyone began to relax, and we chit chatted about everything - other than what had just happened. Julie didn't say too much, except that she was happy about being rescued, and glad she was on her way home. I figured what she and Bill had to talk about was better done in private. We discussed what was next for us, and the three of us agreed we had accomplished what we wanted to, and now was the time to head home.

We had seen a lot, and had some very narrow escapes and close calls. We were lucky no one had gotten hurt. All of that, and the fact we hadn't been arrested yet pointed us in the direction of home. We still had a long way to go, which meant there was plenty of potential for disaster and more run-ins with the authorities.

CHAPTER 19
THE STORM

Now that it has been decided that we are heading back home, the challenge was to make it back safely, and without getting caught. We planned to stop in Key West again to see my friends and then make the final push to Naples. We were going to arrive in Naples about the same time we left - late at night, under the cover of darkness. We had gathered a bunch of small souvenirs from hither and tither and agreed that it would be thoughtful of us to leave a little basket on the boat, as an anonymous token of our appreciation.

Sunrise, on our second day out, there was no sun to be seen. I'd spent years as a boat captain in Florida and watching the weather was second nature. There was something unusual about the sky that morning. The clouds were deep and rather evil looking, stretching out over the whole southeastern sky. It could've been just a tropical disturbance, or possibly a depression. Or worse - it could be a hurricane on the way. The waters were still calm, but it doesn't take long for situations to go from good to bad. If this were a hurricane, the worst place to be is in the eye of it. I'm sure you've seen movies where they show boats in the eye of a storm, and it's sunny and the wind and waters are calm. I can tell you, for a fact, that that's only in the movies. Inside the eye of a hurricane, the seas are at their deadliest, best described as confused and tumultuous. That's the last place we wanted to be. We should have checked the weather before we left, but we didn't have too much of a choice about *when* we left. We were too far offshore to get the NOAA weather reports on the radio. We needed a plan real quick.

By noontime the weather had deteriorated. The wind had picked up to a steady twenty five knots, and the seas were building to six, and sometimes ten feet. The clouds were thick and menacing. They were all moving due north and rotating east to west. Tropical storms rotate counterclockwise. When you look at the rotation, it's just a small arc you can see of a larger circle, and in your mind you have to continue this arc into a big circle and determine where the center is and its movement by which way the clouds are going. It appeared we were on the western side of the rotation, which meant most of the Bahamas was going to get whatever this was, right in their face. The eastern side of the rotation was the worst, so we were somewhat lucky to be where we were. It could have been a lot worse, although hurricanes have a habit of changing course without any notice.

By six o'clock I decided to take the main sail half way down and continue with the forward sail out. I kept the engine running, and told Frank to get out the sea anchor from the compartment in the bow. I told Bill and Julie to secure everything that could move around down below. We didn't want to be hit by flying debris. I didn't tell anyone what my worst fears were. I knew the wind would blow at least 40 knots, and maybe much higher. I didn't want to worry them, but this was going to be some crazy, bad shit. I could only hope we would survive it.

None of us really knew what we should be doing first. The waves were already splashing over the boat. I asked Frank to get the harnesses and made it clear that any-one topside had to be tied on. We couldn't risk anyone falling overboard. The sun had barely set but it looked like it had been down for hours. Frank and I put the sea anchor out over the stern to keep the bow pointed in the right direction. The situation was quickly becoming insane. I told Frank we'd have to get the forward sail down. He began working the winch, furling in the sail. Just at that moment we got broadsided by a large wave.

I looked towards Frank but he was nowhere to be seen. I inched my way to the port rail and there was Frank holding on to his harness for dear life, being dragged along by the boat. I reached over the side and was able to grab hold of his shoulder and pull him up enough that he could grab the rail. After several minutes of adrenalin fueled struggling, Frank fell on the deck. He looked lost and frightened to death. After all we had been through, were we just going to die in the middle of nowhere?

We finally got the forward sail rolled back up. Water was flying all over the boat and we couldn't keep our footing. I was holding onto the wheel for dear life. I put the auto-pilot on a course I thought we should be taking, unhitched myself and Frank, opened up the hatch, and we quickly scrambled below. I closed the hatch, and figured we were either going to somehow survive, or die in the Atlantic.

Bill and Julie were holding on to each other in one corner of the salon. Frank grabbed hold of one end of the sofa and I had my arms wrapped around the mast, and we were all praying. Hours went by, and we were tossed all over the place. There wasn't much to be said, we were all scared to death, and hanging on for dear life. I can remember the stove hanging horizontally in the middle of the boat, and I thought for sure we were going to roll over. Everyone got sick and threw up at least once in the sink.

At some point in the night, sleep must have overtaken us. We were all totally exhausted. I awoke to see the sun coming through one of the portholes, and could immediately tell that the seas had calmed down. I opened the hatch and went topside.

It was truly a miracle. The motor was still plugging along, and the mainsail was still in one piece. The seas had calmed to four feet or less and the wind was just a comfortable breeze. We had somehow survived, when there really wasn't any reason we should have. When your time is up, your time is up, and there is nothing you can do about it. I'm really beginning to believe that old saying... If it's your turn, it's your turn, and if it's not, it's not. I guess it just wasn't our turn. Simple as that.

Everyone came out on deck and took many deep breaths. We all eventually laughed and gave thanks that we had been spared. Frank and I pulled in the sea anchor, unfurled the forward sail, and shut the engine off. It was quiet and beautiful. The ocean can be just like heaven, or just like hell. You have to give it a lot of respect. It's a good thing pain has no memory.

Next, we had to figure out where we were. According to our chart plotter and our GPS, which amazingly still worked, we were about one hundred miles away from where we should have been. We were very close to Cuba. I readjusted our course and headed straight for Key West.

We all slowly came back to normal, and realized how lucky we really were. Frank said, "Time to celebrate! Let's get some bread, cheese, and whatever else we've got and wash it down with some rum!"

In an hour, we were all feeling great. We had conquered Mount Everest!

CHAPTER 20

SAVED

It turned out to be a beautiful day. We did a little trolling, and caught some mahi mahi, which grilled up nicely. I knew that by the end of the next day we would be in Key West and our trip would be coming to an end. Even though we had been through so much, getting back to the old routine didn't seem as sad as you might think. I asked everyone to do whatever they could to get the boat ready for its return to the Naples Yacht Club.

It was almost sundown. Julie was relaxing on the bow when suddenly I heard her scream.

"There's something in the water bobbing up and down in front of us!"

I grabbed the binoculars. Sure enough, about a mile ahead I could see a life raft, on which appeared to be three people waving their arms like crazy. As we got closer I could see that it was a man, a woman, and a child. We lowered the sails and motored up to them. The woman was in tears, holding her child tight, and I imagine they were tears of joy and relief. They looked weathered and confused.

We got them on board, and "happy" would be an understatement of their mood. There were hugs and handshakes all around.

We gave them some food and water, and listened to their horror story.

Seems they were on a three week cruise with their sailboat, far east of us. They knew about the building storm, but as I said, these storms can change course without notice, and they got caught on the wrong side and things went from bad to worse. They did a complete roll over, and their mast and rudder broke. They were taking on water and had no other choice but to launch the lifeboat. They wanted to stay close to the boat which had an EPIRB device for sending out a distress signal, which activated when it went in the water, but their boat sank, and they were quickly blown away by the storm. This was three days ago, and they thought they were goners.

He was a businessman from New York and had chartered the boat they were on from Key West. A bare-boat charter, which meant you could be your own captain. I told him we were headed to Key West and would be happy to take them there. He was more than appreciative, and happier than a pig in shit.

I figured, *what the hell,* and I recounted to him our story, from beginning to end. I told him we would rather have used our own boat, but we didn't have a boat or the means to get one. He seemed in awe, and was amazed how we could have thought of doing something like this, never mind pulling it off, and if we *hadn't* done it we wouldn't have been there to save them.

I told him we were going to Key West for a couple of days and then would be heading back to Naples, dropping the boat off, and getting back to our boring existence. We had a way to go before we were out of the woods.

He said thanks at least a hundred times, and told us he would think of some way to pay us back. I told him he didn't have to do anything to thank us. We were happy to be in the right spot at the right time. Things happen for a reason.

We still had a couple of days left to our voyage, and I gave his family use of the forward stateroom and I would spend my time on deck. We went through the next night without incident, everyone taking their watch without falling asleep.

The next day about noon we had another blip on radar, approaching rapidly from the west, and sure enough I could see with the binoculars a large grey center console heading right for us.

We came about, and they pulled up quickly. I couldn't believe it... shit! It was the same guy in charge that stopped us when we first left Key West!

"Well! Ahoy there! If it isn't the three old geezers!" he said with a slight smile on his face. "I see your family has grown." Before I could say anything, my new friend George - the guy we saved, piped up loudly. "These guys saved my family's life yesterday. They found us floating in our life raft. We were victims of that crazy storm. Our boat sank. If it wasn't for them we might still be floating, and maybe dead. They have been kind enough to take us back to Key West."

The man in charge said, "I see you old geezers have done some good on your voyage. Who is the other woman?"

Bill answered that question, without hesitating. "That's my wife; we picked her up in the Bahamas."

"Okay, okay. I can see you all have had quite the time of it. You have a short trip to Key West. Try not to pick up too many more people. This should give you something to write about when you get home. Take it easy."

They were gone again as fast as they came. A great sense of relief fell over me. It seemed no one had found out about us, and we were now friends- if you want to call it that - with the DEA. Who would have thunk it.

All is well, and tomorrow we will be pulling into Key West.

CHAPTER 21

KEY WEST - AGAIN

I t had been a beautiful sunrise. It was about noon and we were sailing around the western end of Key West, returning to the little island where the transients anchor up. We found a good place to drop anchor, practically the same spot we'd been in before. I asked my new friend George what he wanted to do about getting his family home. He said he planned to just get them ashore and they would stay in a room at the Pier House, and make arrangements for their transportation back home.

I offered him some money, but he said he still had his credit card in his wallet which he hadn't lost. He happened to mention that his company jet would be there to pick his family up the next day. He asked for my mailing information, which I gave to him. We then proceeded to put the dinghy in the water, and made our way to shore.

I let them off at the Pier House Dock. A couple of hugs and good-byes and they were off. Halfway down the dock he called back to me, and said he would be in touch. I said to myself, *wow, company jet...must be nice...bet I never hear from them again.*

I made my way back to the boat, and requested that we do everything we could to clean the boat, and to put everything we no longer needed in garbage bags, which we would take ashore and throw away. I reminded everyone that tomorrow morning we would be on our way, and to expect arriving in Naples at about midnight. We wanted a quick, dark getaway when we got back.

Around four o'clock we had done just about everything we could to clean up. The boat was finally spic n' span, and ship shape, looking exactly as it had the first night we were on it. I suggested we head for shore and try to enjoy our last night on the run. I didn't get any disagreement from anyone, so we all got in the dinghy and headed out to try to find my friends for one last night.

We tied up at the local dinghy center, and crawled across a few of them to the dock. I was hoping to take it easy tonight and be fresh for the final run in the morning. As we turned the corner onto Duval Street, we were overwhelmed by a huge and very noisy crowd. There were people everywhere. Looking up, we saw another banner hanging across the street which said *Welcome to Fantasy Fest!!*

Fantasy Fest is more a celebration of nudity than anything else. A four day long festival, when it's best to leave the kids at home. (Although for a kid, this would have been the best time to be sneaking out of the house - I know I would have.)

It's an alcohol and drug 'slug fest'. It's a sweaty, drunken, people-watching exercise. *Any* excuse is a good excuse to party in Key West, so you can only imagine that this was a good one. Lots of nudity, or at least partial nudity. Mostly women with their bodies painted to make it look like they are wearing something, when they're not. Key West has a way of coming up with these crazy promotions to increase business, and this one draws people from all over the country, and maybe the world. This would *never* happen in Naples!

It was still early, so we decided to head back to the Hog's Breath Saloon to see if my friend Harry was playing tonight. As luck would have it, he was on stage, and already playing. Seems he had booked the early gig. Good, that meant we might be able to do a little partying later on. We sat down and soon caught Harry's eye.

It wasn't long before he took a break and came over to sit down with us. He gave me a sly look and said, "I thought a lot about you guys the last few months, and I had my doubts you were going to make it this far. I see your numbers have increased."

I quickly said, "Yeah, we're surprised too, but we're not out of the woods yet. This is Bill's wife, Julie, who we rescued in the Bahamas. It's all a very long complicated story, but here we are for one last night before we try to get the boat back without any problems. Let's call Martha and get her down here, and go get a bite to eat when you're done playing. We're leaving early in the morning."

Harry called Martha and she agreed to come down shortly. We ordered some beers, and Harry started his last set. It was getting crowded in the bar and you could tell it was *Fantasy Fest*. There were several women in the bar who were wearing nothing to speak of except for some swirls of paint around their nipples. Don't get me wrong I'm not complaining. It was visually stimulating.

Harry asked me if I wanted to play a couple of songs, and since it's not every day these opportunities happen, I said yes. I played my Naples song about Fifth Avenue, which went over big with the crowd. I had one more song up my sleeve that seemed appropriate. It's called "Hey, Little Girl". The first line goes: *Hey little girl, you want some candy? It's not Halloween but that's fine and dandy. Hey little girl, you want to play trick or treat with me?* It's actually a love song, not a pedophile song, but you'd have to hear the rest of it to understand. The whole bar went crazy and that's the way I left them, screaming for more.

Martha showed up and seemed just as surprised as Harry. Neither of them could believe that we were alright *and* had gotten away with our crime, thus far, without being caught. I introduced Martha to Julie, and said what had happened couldn't be explained in the short amount of time we had left. I would just have to write a novel about our adventure, in detail. Maybe even include a few illustrations.

We didn't fool around on our last night. The six of us went over to Louie's Backside for a bite to eat. We wanted to stay above the fray. We'd had enough excitement in the last few months and it was too late in the game to take any unnecessary chances. During dinner I told Harry and Martha the highlights of our trip, and they were impressed. As was I. It was hard to believe all that had transpired. We left them relatively early and went back to the boat. We were excited about getting home.

CHAPTER 22

HOME

We got up early and scoured the boat for any last items that might incriminate us, and left about noon.

Just as we had planned, it was about midnight when we entered the Gordon River. We were old hands now and knew better than to be jumping up and down and making a scene. We were all quiet, and hoping to just get this final couple of miles behind us, get the boat docked and get away without being seen. There wasn't a soul around, and we motored up to the dock we had left from, without lights. All that we didn't want to keep had already been gotten rid of. All we kept was what we could easily carry, which included a few souvenirs. We had cleaned up the boat as best we could and tried to make it look pretty much the same as when we took it.

The only difference was that we had left a small wicker basket, with a few reminders of our travels placed in it, on the table down below. I guess just like a dog pissing on a tree, we wanted the owners to know that someone had been there.

We put the lines on, grabbed our stuff and replaced the lock as we had found it and began our hopefully unnoticed walk back to my condo. Just as we got to the yacht club sure enough the watchman came out the door for his last evening stroll before television and sleep. We smiled and said hello and he did the same. Who would suspect three old geezers or I should say three old geezers, and one old geezer's wife of any wrong doings? I assume he thought we had just gotten off our yacht and were heading home.

We made it back to my condo and Bill, his wife, and Frank quickly departed. We agreed to meet in three days at Badass Coffee. That would give us some time to recover. I went to bed, and laying there I could still feel my inner ear trying to get used to not moving about. I felt I was still rolling side to side on the boat, but nevertheless, I quickly fell into a deep sleep.

CHAPTER 23

HITTING IT BIG

Three days later, shortly after sunrise, I had only walked a couple of hundred yards when I could feel the first drop of perspiration slide down the side of my face. I rounded the corner of Third Street and sure enough there was Bill, Julie, and Frank sitting in front of Badass Coffee. I felt like all that had happened was a dream, except that Julie was also sitting there. She was apparently part of the gang now.

Bill yelled, "Morning Cap, I see you're still breathing!"

I yelled back, "You gotta get it while you can."

I went into Badass Coffee, got my raisin bagel with cream cheese, and my decaf coffee, and went out and sat next to Frank, who was blowing his perfect little smoke rings into the heavy moisture laden air. We looked at each other and just smiled. After a short while Julie said that she and Bill had been talking and decided that they were going to try to work it out.

Julie spoke up, "I know my yardstick is getting shorter just like you guys and sometimes you forget what's important. You lose track of what's real in life, and what really means something. As she looked at Bill she said, "It's important to know who really loves you."

I think they both have learned an important lesson and I hope it works out for them. Frank and I are still going it solo and I don't see that changing anytime soon.

We sat there for another hour or so talking about our adventures when a couple sat down at the next table. I could overhear the man say he thought something wasn't right with their sailboat. Seems they had just gotten back in town, were going to stay a couple of weeks, and he had checked on their sailboat and found a basket of shells and what-nots in the cabin below. He was asking his wife if she had any idea of how it got there, and of course we knew she didn't. I knew then that we had made it back just in time. It must be destiny. We all grinned wildly, and of course didn't say a thing.

Unknown to anyone, I had a very important announcement, and a secret I couldn't hide any longer. I smiled, and let the cat out of the bag.

"I have something to say and you're going to want to hear this, so be quiet till I've finished. You know the people we saved after the storm? Well, they have shown us their gratitude. You remember it was obvious he had some money, especially since he had a jet coming to pick him and his family up in Key West? Yesterday I received a letter from him. I didn't call you right away because I knew we were meeting today. Inside the envelope was a check for three million dollars. Yes, THREE MILLION DOLLARS!" Nobody said a word, you could have heard a frog fart. Then an onslaught of *holy shit, no money down, wow, I can't believe it, this can't be real.* I reassured them that it was in fact real, and the next morning we should meet at the bank and take care of business. Everyone naturally agreed.

When everyone calmed down, I looked at Frank and said, "I think I'm going to write a book about this, and Bill you're an artist, maybe you could do the cover. We have to think about our next adventure. Frank, don't you have a pilot's license?" We all laughed until we cried. I'm sure the people next to us thought we were crazy, and they might be right.

Now we were three old geezers with three million bucks, and looking for our next adventure.

Bombs Away!!!!

CHAPTER 24

IN HINDSIGHT

Six months had gone by, and everything was slowly falling back into the same routine. Early mornings at Bad Ass Coffee and the resuming of our typical conversation about the lack of adventure in our lives. The excitement of our jaunt into the unknown world of calculated risk has waned and we are back in our short yardstick mode. Julie and Bill are seemingly getting along quite well, but pain has no memory, and the workings of the mind are impossible to figure out. I feel their breakup a second time is inevitable. Bill and Frank are again meeting near the restrooms by the pier in the evenings and watching the scenery walk by.

Of course, we all have some money now; in fact you could say we're rich. Frank bought a fancy new car, and Bill indulged in the purchase of a small boat for cruising around the backwaters. My money is just burning a hole in my pocket. I have no intention of dying with a lot of money in the bank - I just don't know what to do with it.

Happiness seems to be flighty - here one minute and gone the next. My mind keeps getting in the way. *What if... what if...* Thoughts that drive me crazy. I don't really want to be a Buddhist, sitting around meditating my life away looking for nirvana. I still want some real world, dysfunctional, crazy shit going on! We live in an era of instant gratification. There's no way around it. The old saying about "happiness being something to do, something to look forward to, and someone to love" seems to be right on the money. I don't have a member of the opposite sex to love right now, and I may never have, but I love my buddies and that will have to do. Having something to do and something to look forward to - well, that's up to me. I know that the boys and I are going to have to break out again soon.

Richard Perron is a coast guard licensed boat captain who in the late 1980s enjoyed a successful career as a florist in New England.

Now living in Naples, Florida, Perron is a singer-songwriter and musician who performs throughout the Naples area and has several CDs to his credit. Further information can be found at www.reverbnation.com/captainrichard.

Made in the USA
Middletown, DE
04 January 2023

17435125R00076